Summer
with
Mary-Lou

WITHDRAWN
FOR SALE

JN 03897752

Summer
with
Mary-Lou

STEFAN CASTA

Translated from the Swedish
by Tom Geddes

Andersen Press • London

First published in 2005 by
Andersen Press Limited,
20 Vauxhall Bridge Road, London SWIV 2SA

© 1997 by Stefan Casta
Original title: *Fallet Mary-Lou*
First published in Swedish by
Bokförlaget Opal, Bromma
English translation © 2005 by Tom Geddes

All rights reserved. No part of this publication may be reproduced,
stored in a retrieval system, or transmitted in any form or by any
means, electronic, mechanical, photocopying, recording or
otherwise, without the written permission of the publisher.

British Library Cataloguing in Publication Data available
ISBN 1 84270 246 7

LINCOLNSHIRE COUNTY COUNCIL	
03897752	
PETERS	£5.99
26-Apr-05	TA

Typeset by FiSH Books, London WC1
Printed and bound in Great Britain by Bookmarque Ltd.,
Croydon, Surrey

IT was the Stockholm rush hour. And mine too. We'd had a drawing lesson outside in the afternoon and I'd stayed behind when the others left and made myself late. I got off the underground at Skanstull and threaded my way up through the crowds.

I cast a glance as usual at the window of the fish shop. They were advertising fresh rock salmon, and as I crossed over Göta Street I started wondering what you do with it: poach it or fry it?

I was roused from my daydream by two guys in an open-top Peugeot 204 tooting at me. I skipped nimbly on to the kerb. I had my big portfolio under my arm, full of drawings and sketches that I was taking home.

I remember thinking: it'll soon be summer. Because that was the first convertible I'd seen this year. It was the middle of April, one of the first warm days, with a pale silvery sun shining over the city.

Perhaps that was why I didn't see anything – because I was thinking about summer. My head was already full of it. Of plans. And a tiny nagging worry.

Suddenly there was a bang. And the whole pavement was full of me. Of me and a million white angels fluttering about me.

I was on all fours looking round foolishly. I could feel a stabbing pain in my right foot. Realised that the angels were my sheets of paper blowing all over the street on the wind. Saw a heap of library books spilling across the pavement. Became aware of a girl in a wheelchair right in front of me. She was obviously furious.

'You might look where you're going,' she snarled.

People were stopping and making pathetic attempts to catch the flying sheets of paper. I crawled about on my hands and knees picking up the books. I could see it was my own fault. That I must have gone smack into the wheelchair when I jumped up on the kerb. It felt as if I'd collided with the mobile library. I stood up.

'I'm so sorry,' I said piling up the books on the wheelchair.

Then, as she turned her face towards me with a shy, sad look, I saw who it was I'd literally bumped into.

'Mary-Lou!' I cried.

She was dressed in really smart clothes. Her brown hair was neatly trimmed and shaped. She seemed like a different person. It was obvious that she hadn't recognised me either. It wouldn't have surprised me if she'd blanked it all out of her memory.

'Adam!' I said. 'Adam from the country!'

Then it seemed to come back to her.

'Great to see you again,' she said.

'I've been thinking of ringing you for ages,' I said.

But I didn't say why I hadn't.

A car braked to a halt. My papers were causing mayhem.

'Quick, before they blow down to the main road,' she said.

I ran out into the road, half-crouching. My foot was agony. Most of the sheets were in the gutter. I gathered them up one by one and some small boys lent a hand. I limped back to Mary-Lou, who was watching my progress.

People were barging into us as they tried to push past. She gave me a hesitant glance, as if wondering what we ought to do next. I looked at the books lying higgledy-piggledy on her lap.

'Let's go in here,' I said, indicating McDonald's.

She started rolling her chair towards the entrance. I was walking by her side but there was a stream of people coming out so it seemed better for me to go first. We went over to the window just inside the door. She dried the books with a napkin. There were two jackdaws on the pavement outside, staring at us with their piercing eyes. I had a great desire to draw them, but this wasn't the moment.

I focused on Mary-Lou instead. Saw the little details I'd missed earlier: the green leather bag with the word Mulberry on it, the dark blue silk scarf elegantly looped beneath the collar of her light coat. She reminded me of an air hostess. She had *upper class* written all over her. Though I was well enough acquainted with her to know that she belonged elsewhere.

'How's your vertigo nowadays?' she asked when she'd finished arranging the books on her lap.

'Obviously no better,' I said with a laugh.

She studied me thoughtfully, as if trying to figure something out.

'You've changed,' she said.

'You've changed even more,' I replied.

Then I didn't know what else to say. Nor did she. We fell silent. So I decided I'd tell her about my plans.

'I'm going to stay in the country all summer by myself. Live on fish and things.'

'Will they let you?' she asked.

'Sure. I mostly live on my own here in Stockholm anyway. My dad's almost always away working. I take care of myself. Myself and my dad, when he's at home.'

There was another silence.

'You could come out!' I suddenly exclaimed. 'I'd actually wondered about phoning you to suggest it.'

'I'm not sure I'd want to.'

'You could think about it.'

She nodded.

'Do you live near here?' I asked, surprised that I'd never encountered her before.

She shook her head.

'I'm meeting a friend. Mona. We're going to sing in St Sophia's Church. But I'm far too early.'

'My grandmother's buried there,' I said.

She opened the leather bag, took out a gold-coloured card and handed it to me.

It was a visiting card. Mary-Lou Arvnell. An address on the east side of the city: 13 Sibylle Street. A telephone number.

'Has your mum remarried?'

Mary-Lou nodded.

'But your dad's still got the farm?'

She nodded again. I thought about all she must have gone through. How long ago was it? Three years? Of course it was, I knew perfectly well. If there was anything I was certain of, it was that: it would be three years ago this summer.

'How's it going?' I said, with the barest nod at the wheelchair.

She shrugged her shoulders. Then said in a nonchalant tone, 'It's okay. I'm getting used to it. When we moved here I said I'd fallen off the Eiffel Tower. So they'd leave me alone at school. I was awful, Mona says.' She laughed. Then she repeated, 'But it's okay now. It's no big deal any more.'

I thought this didn't quite ring true. I glanced at my watch and saw I had to get going. It was Wednesday. It was the final of the junior indoor hockey league. I had to go to the supermarket for crisps and a crate of fizzy drink and then get home in time to make something more or less edible for my father. He was due back from Amman.

It struck me that it was really my father and her parents who had been friends. That was how we got to know each other. I had an idea my father and her mother might also have been in touch since.

'My dad's coming home from Jordan tonight,' I said.

'Is he still travelling just as much?'

'Even more!'

I slipped the gold visiting card into the pocket of my jeans and said goodbye.

'Think about it,' I said.

5

'I can't imagine I'd be allowed to come,' she said.
'I'll phone you,' I said.

Which I did a few days later. It was a Saturday. She was watching TV. We talked for quite a while. It sounded as if she remembered better now. She said she'd spoken to her mother about me and that I should pass on greetings to my father.

She said how weird it was that we should bump into each other like that. I said it was the sort of thing that was always happening to me.

I carried on phoning her. Sometimes I got the answerphone and just hung up. She never rang me. Sometimes she sounded upset or angry. We didn't talk for so long then.

I asked whether she'd given my suggestion any further thought. She said she didn't know yet. But I got the feeling that she understood.

1

The screeching of the gulls woke me up early. I lay there listening under my red blanket: *Kyow gah-gah-gaaah*. I could hear the distant echo of a fishing boat on its way out or in and thought the engine sounded like an anxious heart pounding hard and fast against the soft regular breathing of the waves. I tried to keep in time with the waves. Steady, little heart. I breathed slowly in and out, in and out, in and out. Like the waves.

Kept drifting back to sleep.

Sunshine and blue sky, I would write in my diary later. Later when I woke up. *Sunshine and blue sky, 19°, light south-westerly wind.*

I put a saucepan of water on the stove for tea, opened the door and went out for a pee in the tall willowherb by the side of the house. The sun was shining on the back of my neck. It was midday. I gazed over the lake. A duck came gliding past under the jetty with a line of ducklings behind her as if in tow. She looked up at me. I counted seven, but then I saw a straggler paddling along a bit after the others. 'Hurry up, little bird,' I whispered.

The water was boiling when I came in, and I turned it off and dropped in a teabag. I cut three slices of bread and spread them with cream cheese but no butter.

I sat on the wooden bench in front of the cottage. You could smell the woods. Some yachts were making slow headway in the gentle breeze. This was my everyday life. Wind and waves.

A wagtail came bouncing across the grass and I threw it some breadcrumbs, but then it decided to make a few quick hops down to the water's edge.

I heard clucking, and stood up and stretched my sleepy body and went over to the old Volvo Duett estate car to feed Siv and Ruth. I took a couple of handfuls of corn from the wooden tub in the outhouse.

'Here you are, then, come and get it,' I encouraged them.

They tumbled out of the back doors of the car, cackling irritably as I scattered the seed through the wire netting surrounding it. They pecked up the corn greedily.

'Have you laid any eggs today?' I asked. But they were too busy to chat, so I opened the wire-netting door and slipped into the chicken run. Siv retreated and gave me a suspicious glance, but when she saw that Ruth went on eating she too resumed her belated breakfast. I checked to make sure the water-dispenser was full.

Then I opened the front door and was delighted to find one brown egg on the passenger seat. It still felt warm when I picked it up and I slid it gently into my pocket.

'Good girls,' I said, closing the door quietly and leaving the chicken run.

One egg, I wrote in my diary. I put it in the big wooden egg rack in the larder. One egg in a rack that could take thirty looked a bit desolate. But Siv and Ruth needed time, time to get used to me. Everything out here needed time to get used to things. Myself most of all.

*

I took my sketchpad and strolled over to the conifer woods. It was a real enchanted forest with fir trees hundreds of years old. It would take several people to get their arms round any of the trunks. But there were also sunny glades and marshy areas white with cotton grass. I sat cross-legged on the ground and sketched some buttercups that looked unusual to me. The flowers seemed frayed and imperfect. Some had five yellow petals, others seemed to have none at all. I knew that this unfinished impression was typical of the species called goldilocks. I wrote the name underneath, *Ranunculus auricomus, 14th June*.

Then I noticed the short-stemmed white flowers on the ground, so dense that they were like a carpet over the glade. Little white flowers gleaming everywhere with green trefoil leaves. I was glad because I knew they were wild strawberries. To think that they were still here!

I wrote it in my diary later: *There'll be a lot of strawberries in the enchanted forest*.

In the evening I sat at the big table by the window and watched the lake smooth over after yet another day of boats and gulls. I went out and closed the car doors on Siv and Ruth. The wind had swung round to the south-east. It was freshening up a bit and the fir trees were whispering to one another.

'Goodnight, girls,' I called, but got no response. I stood there in silence and heard the sound of sleeping from inside the vehicle. So I came back indoors.

I shut the door of the cottage and after a momentary

hesitation turned the key in the lock. Don't ask me why. Probably just a bad habit from the city.

I woke up in the middle of the night. I had no idea how long I'd been asleep. The rain was pattering hard on the roof and at first I thought that was what had woken me. Then I heard it again. A muffled explosion. From somewhere outside, quite close.

I thought of Siv and Ruth because there were foxes in the woods, but the noise hadn't come from the direction of the chicken coop.

I lay listening for a while. My heart was like a fishing boat again, a fast dull throb.

I sat up in bed. There it was again: *Boom*. I tried to see out of the window. It was dark. I couldn't even see where the land ended and the water began.

At that very moment the blackness of night was split open by a long white gash, as if someone had undone a luminous zip stretching from high into the sky to the surface of the sea. In the vivid glare I could see everything that only an instant before I hadn't been able to see at all: the boat at the jetty, the empty beach, the shape of the forest, the hens' Volvo Duett.

I held my breath. I managed a count of three before it came again: *Boom*.

I crawled back under the bedclothes. Pulled the red blanket up. Right over my head. When I was little I was afraid of lightning. But I wasn't little now.

*

When I was little my dad and I and Britt Börjesson used to stay in the cottage.

We had great summers here, especially when Britt didn't turn up. I would be running in and out of the water for days on end, the way small boys do. I loved going in the water. If you're in the water as much as that you'll get webbed feet, Britt used to say. And then she would burst out laughing.

I believed it at first. Children can be really stupid. One day she seized me by the arm and dragged me out to the end of the jetty. Then she made me jump in. She shouted at me to swim to the shore, with my webbed feet. Then she ran round to the beach and stood there shrieking with mirth while I flailed my arms and yelled that I was drowning. That was when I realised she didn't know anything about children.

I think that was what prevented me ever learning to swim. I developed some kind of phobia of the water. I would stand stock-still in the lake. They could have moored the boat to me.

I started going fishing. Found a place where a small stream of brown marsh water flowed into the lake. Right at the mouth of the stream I could catch perch that were so dark green they were virtually black.

Britt asked where I caught them. Miles away. Beyond Norden Farm. Way out on their spit, I told her. It was the other end of the world. As far as you could go. But I don't know whether she actually ever went there.

In the evenings I would lie in bed listening to Britt sipping her sparkling wine and laughing her raucous guffaws.

I would think, now comes the thunderstorm. But there would be no lightning. Just the constant rumbling.

I didn't know that laughter could sound so unpleasant. That it could make me feel so irritable. They say that the eyes are the windows of the soul. But a person's laughter can be too. Though I didn't understand that until a lot later, when Britt Börjesson and I settled our scores.

When I woke up the sky was clear. It was a bright whitish-blue. I had slept for a long time again, too long, but I blamed the night's storms.

I put on the water for tea, went out to pee in the willowherb and ambled over to the chicken coop.

Siv and Ruth also seemed to have slept badly. They came waddling reluctantly to the door when I called them but wouldn't come down until I'd thrown in two handfuls of grain.

No eggs today – but who was going to feel like laying an egg after a night like that?

Once back inside I took the saucepan off the hotplate to make the tea. I cut two slices of bread and squeezed caviar from a tube on them. When I poured the tea into the cup I noticed that it was stone cold. At first I couldn't suss it out. Then I splashed a few drops of water on the hotplate. That was cold too. I turned on the light switch but knew in advance I was wasting my time. The electricity was off. I wondered whether I could fix it by changing a fuse or whether it was a power cut from the transformer over the other side of the bay.

13°, clear, moderate north-easterly. No electricity after the thunderstorm in the night, I wrote.

The weather improved as the day wore on, and the sun suddenly broke through when I was sitting out on the jetty. I took off my sweater to let my pale body warm up.

I liked sitting there. The jetty was built on huge angular boulders and sturdy piles sunk into the bed of the lake. There were wide planks nailed across the top, black with tar and white with gull droppings. It was big enough to take a canal boat. Dad sometimes used to joke about that. We might find the *Diana* or the *Juno* moored at the jetty one morning, he would say. But apart from the occasional pleasure yacht sheltering from a sudden squall, there had never been anything larger than Britt's double-ended traditional Vättern working boat, or *snipa*, as it was known.

I squinted out across the lake, sketching at random. With soft pencil strokes I outlined the bay that cut deep into the landscape and was bordered by two long green arms. One arm was where I was sitting. That was my peninsula. There was nothing but forest and glades and marsh here. And our cottage, of course.

The opposite peninsula was more open and light. There was a farm there called Norden, and the wheatfields shone like pale yellow picnic rugs between meandering tracks.

I turned my attention again to the lake itself and tried to reproduce the shapes of the islands that lay like boats at anchor out in the middle. The nearest one resembled a whale. That was The Maiden. It was bare. Just stones and rocks and hillocks, and thousands of nesting gulls.

The other island looked like a loaf. That was Fjuk. It was really several separate islands, but you couldn't see that from here. They all merged into one. People said you never knew where you were with Fjuk. Sometimes it was just a shimmering mirage hovering several metres above the water.

I had been gazing at those islands ever since I was a kid. I had dreamt about them. Imagined myself sailing to them and exploring them. But I had never set foot there. We're not boat people, Dad and I.

I examined my rough sketches but was not happy with the results. I had tried drawing the islands many times. Yet they always eluded me. There was something about them I couldn't capture. Something not visible to the eye. I had always felt attracted to that, trying to put the invisible into a picture. Moods, feelings and the like. Artists talk about a special light they're trying to catch. But I was trying to capture what couldn't be seen. I wanted to learn to draw what words can't express. I said that to Gunilla Fahlander in an art class once. 'That's good, Adam,' she replied. 'We should set our sights on the stars.'

The net was in the outhouse. Whoever had used it last must have been in a real rush, because it was all tangled up in a big white plastic bowl. Just as it had been hauled out of the water. Not washed, cleaned or untangled. If you didn't know it was a fishing net, you'd never have guessed.

After some hesitation I picked up the bowl and carried it out to the garden. I put it down by the veranda and eventually managed to find a loose end and begin the laborious task of unravelling it all.

I hooked the end to a nail on the veranda and unwound the net over towards the wash-stand by the sour-cherry bushes. There I turned and walked back towards the house. The net was in a sorry state. Large parts of it resembled a twisted rope. And the sections that I got to lie flat and unravel were so torn that I had to laugh. But I knew it could be fixed. Even if it took for ever. It could. Everything can. Everything, if you really want it to be.

By evening I was overcome by an almighty hunger and remembered I hadn't eaten since the morning. I could see a light in the cottage, so I knew the electricity must be on again. I went indoors and through to the spacious larder and let my eyes roam along the shelves of tins. I took a tin of haricot beans. I put the old frying pan with the high sides on one of the hotplates and cut up some bacon into little squares. I sawed round half the lid of the beans with the mini tin-opener and then bent the rest back. When the bacon pieces looked more or less done I poured the beans in and let it all heat through gently.

I ate straight from the frying pan, down on the jetty. The sun was in the west now, almost mid-way between The Maiden and Fjuk. But it was none too warm, so I put my sweater on.

When I'd eaten I lay on my stomach and dipped the

15

pan into the clear cold water and washed it with one hand. A shoal of perch darted off in fright among the boulders of the jetty.

'Don't be scared,' I whispered. 'It's only me. It's Adam.'

They emerged again a few moments later nibbling tentatively at the remnants of food I'd left. I lay there watching the shimmering green fish until I realised that I wasn't looking at them any more but at another image moving in the distorting mirror of water. The reflection of Adam. The blurred image of Adam O.

'Come in and eat now, Adam!'

I can hear Britt's voice from up at the cottage. She doesn't sound the way mothers should sound. It's not a friendly invitation. There's not a trace of warmth in her voice. She could be shouting anything. Britt always speaks to me in the same tone. 'Adam, brush your teeth! Good night, Adam! Adam, quick march!'

But instead of obeying orders I run off in the opposite direction. I hare off into the enchanted forest. In among the dense bushes that take me into their embrace and hide me from Britt Börjesson.

As dusk fell I went in and sat down at the long wooden table. A bumblebee was buzzing angrily as it kept bashing itself against the windowpane so I got up to let it out. It was ages since anyone had opened the window and I had to push really hard before it would budge. A big flake of paint on the outside went with it. The bee flew out to freedom and was swallowed up in the darkness.

I closed the window and turned on the light and went to get the book on perspective drawing that Gunilla Fahlander had insisted I should read this summer. Despite being completely on my own, I had difficulty concentrating. Books like this had never really interested me. They were too dry. I doubted whether it was possible to learn to draw from a book. I couldn't anyway. And this wasn't the way I wanted to draw, it wasn't technical proficiency I was after. Even though I could see that you had to master that too. You have to know how to do it to be able to progress beyond it, Gunilla had said when she lent me the book.

A sudden knocking at the door made me nearly jump out of my skin. It wasn't particularly loud, but in the silence it sounded like pistol shots.

I didn't know what to do. My first thought was to try and escape. Maybe through the kitchen window? I was afraid, though I must have known there was little reason to be.

By the time it was repeated I had calmed down a bit. Whoever was out there must already have peered into the lighted room anyway.

'Who is it?' I shouted cautiously.

'It's Björn . . . Björn Arvnell.'

I went into the porch, switched on the exterior light and opened the door.

The man outside blinked in the sudden glare. He was dressed in jeans and wooden clogs and a shabby brown cord jacket. Under the jacket he was wearing a striped pullover with a zip at the neck. It made him look bigger than he was. He had a battered cap on his head that must once have been plaid but was now a faded pale grey from sun and grime. His weasely face was covered in a growth of stubble. He bared his teeth in an attempt at a smile.

'I saw your light was on,' he said. 'I thought it must be you.'

I said nothing. Just nodded.

'Are you staying long?'

'I'm not really sure. Possibly.'

'You've sorted the net out.' He gestured in the direction of the faint misty line running across the garden. 'You made a good job of it.'

'There's not much of it left.'

'I nearly tripped over it anyway,' said Björn with an abrupt laugh.

A painful silence ensued. I didn't know what else to say. Nor did Björn, obviously. I thought he looked tired.

'You've grown a lot,' he said finally. 'How old are you now, seventeen?'

'Fifteen,' I corrected him. 'How are things with you, then?' I asked in an attempt to be polite.

'Oh, I get by. The fishing is dire, of course, but it's been like that for years. I'm farming fish now. Steelhead salmon. You've probably seen the pools.'

I nodded. The newly dug pools scarred the landscape on the peninsula opposite.

'And farming is the way it is. Though at least there's been some rain this year.'

'Where are all the cows?'

18

'Gone to the abattoir. They got to be too much work. I can't manage everything single-handed.'

Then I plucked up the courage to ask, 'And . . . Mary-Lou, how . . . is she okay too?'

He nodded.

'As far as I know.'

I didn't want to ask anything else. I wondered if I ought to mention that I'd met her. But somehow I didn't.

'Won't you come in?' I suggested instead.

'Thanks, but I just nipped over to make sure you were all right. You know I promised Britt I'd keep an eye on things.'

'Yes.'

'You're feeding the chickens?'

'Of course.'

'Fine, so I can stop bothering about them for the time being.'

He stood down off the granite step and turned to go.

'Have fun, then,' he said.

When he was halfway across the garden I called out, 'Are you going to tell Britt I'm here?'

He stopped. Scratched himself under the peak of his cap.

'No, I don't suppose there's any need to. Since it's you.'

I closed the door and heaved a sigh of relief. I was glad he hadn't asked any more questions.

I went to bed, but found it hard to get to sleep. I think I lay there restlessly for a couple of hours before I suddenly remembered that I'd forgotten to shut Siv and Ruth in. I leapt up and pulled on my jeans and sweater and ran barefoot into the garden.

I went into the ramshackle chicken run and stood by the car to listen. When I thought I could hear the hens' sleepy clucking I closed the rear doors.

'Sleep tight, girls.'

I walked back pensively over the dewy grass. My conversation with Björn had stirred up a lot of things. A lot of what had happened before.

Now it felt as if it had been just last week. Everything was the same. Everything was as it had been then. There were the same smells in the garden. The same wet grass on my bare feet. The same muted sigh of the fir trees in the forest and the gentle breathing of the lake. Everything I loved so much. It was only me who had changed.

'Adam, come on!'

I'm on my knees among tussocks of grass in the dank wood. I've seen some flowers, some small green and white bell-shaped flowers that I've never noticed before. They are hanging like a string of white pearls on bare stalks. Almost like lilies of the valley. Yet not like them at all. They're not like anything else I've ever seen. I'm surprised that such pretty flowers can grow so deep inside the wood, among berries and ferns and moss.

'Adam!'

I quickly break off a stalk and start running in the direction of my father and Britt. I gallop through the mounds of sedge, pretending I'm a wild horse being pursued by a pack of wolves. Snorting with energy and feigned terror I dash into the safe haven between my father's legs and in my haste collide with Britt's trug and send blueberries flying everywhere.

'Be careful, Adam!'

'Look what I've found! Are they pimpernels?'

I hand the white forest flower proudly to my dad and he takes it and inspects it. A smile plays at the corner of his mouth.

'It's not a pimpernel, Adam, but it's a beautiful flower.'

I smile too, pleased to have found so fine a specimen for him.

Then he takes out his magnifying glass from his breast pocket to inspect the various parts of the flower. He does it to lend greater significance to my discovery. He pretends not to notice that Britt is shuffling her feet in impatience.

'It's a wintergreen,' he says with an approving nod at me. 'See this bare upright stalk, it's typical of the pyrola family.'

He gives me the flower back and I put it carefully along the edge of my basket because I want to press it and add it to our collection. Pyrola media.

To my and my father's collection.

I was woken early by the rain drumming on the roof. I went over to the window. The downpour was making the lake boil. The drops seemed to plunge below the surface and be thrown up again in a pattern I knew so well and yet never tired of watching. I put the water on for tea. There was only a crust left of the loaf, and it reminded me of a piece of tree bark. I stuffed it in my pocket.

It was warm outside, and the sun was trying to break through the clouds. We'd had the worst of the weather. It would be a fine day.

Siv and Ruth declined to come out in the rain, so I laid their corn in a little heap inside the car.

'You can have some bread, too,' I said, rubbing the last of the loaf between my palms. They pecked at the crumbs as they fell. I searched for eggs, on the seats and in the luggage-space, but couldn't find any. I gave them a mild ticking off.

I found some peach halves in the larder and ate them straight out of the tin. The sweet pieces of fruit melted succulently in my mouth. Then I drank my tea sitting on the step at the front of the cottage, where a small projecting roof kept off the last drops of rain. The sun had broken through now and was shining down like angel hair over the fields on the other side of the bay.

I started thinking about Mary-Lou again.

I wondered how she was. Whether she had changed her mind and would want to come back out here. Like me.

It's Sunday. The Swedish blue and yellow flag hanging slackly from the top of the white flagpole. A cluster of well-dressed people round the table, drinking coffee and eating.

I'm walking along the path between the flowerbeds. It ends at a circle of newly laid black slabs with an almost mirror-like surface. I know it's black granite because I watched Björn laying them. He got them in some strange barter deal that he often goes in for. In the middle of the

22

stone circle stands the old cherry tree, groaning with fruit.

That's where I find her. She's sitting up in the tree and has been observing me all the time. She's not dressed in her best clothes like me but in jeans and a red T-shirt. She has a yellow cap on her head with the name of nearby Odal on it.

'Hello, Adam,' she says.

She is weighing me up. She tosses her head and swings her long brown hair.

'Hi,' I reply.

'Come and join me,' she says.

My attention shifts from Mary-Lou to the cherries. I've never seen so many before. At home we just have wild cherries that are so sour you have to spit them out.

I hesitate. Think of my clothes. But then follow her example and start clambering up the rough trunk.

Above me I can see Mary-Lou climbing even higher. Stepping from branch to branch as if it were no more than a ladder.

She comes to a halt, sitting on the highest branches that will bear her weight.

'Faster,' she calls.

I climb doggedly on. Avoiding looking down and keeping my eyes on the trunk. On one of the branches I come upon a golden lump of something or other.

'What's this?' I ask, grateful for an excuse to pause.

'It's only resin,' she says.

I prod the solid yellow-brown mass.

'It looks like gold,' I say.

We're sitting near the top of the tree now, like two baby eaglets. Mary-Lou's birthday party is going on below us. The gravel drive is freshly raked and full of cars. Mary-Lou's grandmother has arrived from her sheltered accommodation. She's nearly ninety with white hair and the same inquisitive eyes as Mary-Lou. Björn's bald red pate is gleaming in the sun. I'm always surprised by it, wondering if it can be normal to lose your hair so early. I can hear him telling a funny story and as he finishes Britt's shrill laugh comes floating through the garden. I make a face at Mary-Lou. But it's as if it has nothing to do with us. As if Britt can't reach me up here.

'They're very good,' I say, focusing on the cherries in my hand.

Mary-Lou's eyes are on me.

'You're feeling giddy, aren't you?'

I nod vigorously, still looking no further than the cherries.

'Yes I am.'

'You're really brave, climbing up regardless,' she says.

I feel proud. I make an attempt to look beyond my hand, but I only manage a glimpse of the black stone slabs beneath the tree before I feel my head starting to spin and I have to steady myself by clutching at a branch.

'Shall I tell you what I can see from here?'

I nod.

Mary-Lou stands up in the tree. I am afraid for her and grab her by the leg.

'Are you mad?' I whisper.

'Huh, this is nothing compared to the Eiffel Tower.'

'Have you been up that?'

'No, but I'm going to. My dad says we're going there.'

'Can you see Fjuk?'

'Yes. And The Maiden. And your cottage. There are three foxes round your chicken run. And the front tyre of your bike is flat.'

'You fibber! There's no way you can see anything like that!'

Mary-Lou bursts out laughing.

'You've got to have imagination, Adam!'

I cycled to the shop in the afternoon. I pedalled in a leisurely fashion along the unsurfaced winding road breathing in the familiar scents of wheatfields and peas. At the bend after the bus stop I saw cornflowers along the edge of the field and regretted not bringing my sketchpad. I stopped and picked a bunch and put them on my carrier.

There were no customers in the shop and I mooched a little aimlessly around the shelves. I picked up two loaves. Toyed with a box of half-a-dozen eggs but put it back.

'Nothing else?' asked Mr Rosén, looking up from his newspaper. He turned the loaves over and keyed in the price on his till.

'No, thanks. Oh, yes – batteries. Ordinary torch batteries. Two.'

He took down two batteries from the display by the counter. He was about to hand them to me, but stopped himself and said, 'Surely, it's . . . Adam, isn't it? Haven't seen you in ages.'

'No, I replied, 'it was quite a time ago.'

'You'll be staying for a while?'

I nodded.

'Yes.'

'So, how's life in the big city?'

'Oh, it's okay.'

I put two twenty-crown notes on the counter. He took them and gave me a handful of coins in change.

'Pass on my greetings,' he said.

I nodded and opened the door. Then I remembered I wanted a phone card too. Having got it, I said goodbye to Mr Rosén once more and crossed to the public telephone opposite. I went into the box and dialled and let it ring for several minutes without getting any response.

The cornflowers on my carrier were already wilting as I cycled the last bit. There's no path right up to the house. At least not a proper one. The dirt road comes to an end with a sharp left-hand bend going off down to the holiday cottages. But I pedalled straight on following two almost invisible wheel tracks leading over the open pastureland. Once there used to be cows lying under the trees and your tyres would give off a rank smell from the cow dung you'd ridden through.

I rowed with unhurried strokes, rested the oars in the air and let the boat glide for a moment before bracing my feet again and dipping the oars. It was a long boat and

26

an effort to row. But it was stable and if you just kept rowing steadily it would move quite willingly across the water. You just had to keep it going. The worst thing was the lifejacket, which was really bugging.

I rowed out parallel with the spit, in a westerly direction. When I came to the big rocks at the end of the point, I turned south. I rested the oars on the stern thwart and looked for the first landmark ashore.

I couldn't see it. Perhaps everything had altered so much that the old landmarks just weren't there. Or maybe it was my bad memory.

I decided to cast the net anyway and threw in the red plastic float. I gave a few pulls on the oars to set the boat in motion and stood up and started unwinding the net from its plastic spool in time with the movement. I was glad no one could see me because the net was not a pretty sight. Despite doing what I could to patch it up, large parts were still badly torn. It just looked as if I was laying out a lengthy fishing line.

The net came to an end surprisingly quickly and the last plastic float bobbed away over the surface as soon as I let it go. I glanced up at the sky but saw no sign of any banks of cloud gathering on the horizon. It would probably be reasonable weather tomorrow.

20° and sunny after a rainy night. Light south-easterly breeze, I wrote that evening.

I fell asleep quite early but was jolted awake by the book on perspective falling on my face.

'No, Mary-Lou! Stop it!'

I'm standing with my arms tightly hugging my chest. The water is up to my knees. I've been standing in the same place for so long that the never-ending ridges on the sandy bottom have flattened out under my feet. The water is cold and my legs are hurting.

Britt is lying on the beach sunbathing. She is topless and her breasts are pointing in two different directions, as if scanning the deserted beach for handsome blokes. Dad is in a deckchair in the shade of the alder trees reading a newspaper.

A wagtail is scampering along the beach. I've been watching it for a while and seen how fast it snaps up mosquitoes at the water's edge.

The wagtail flies off in fright when Mary-Lou comes charging over. She's wearing a red two-piece bathing costume and splashing her way through the water. She's raising her knees so high that water is spraying up all around her. She's running straight towards me and passes so close that the cold water cascades all over me.

I yell to high heaven and turn round to keep her in view. She flings herself headlong, goes under and surfaces with a snort. Then she fixes me with her penetrating eyes.

'No!' I shout. 'Stop it! Don't!'

But Mary-Lou won't stop. She laughs with delight and rushes up again. This time she comes right up to me and pulls away my hands that are firmly clenched across my chest. She dances round me till I fall over.

'Stop it!' I cry. 'Leave me alone!'

I hear Britt cackling on the beach.

I race out of the water up the beach and snatch Mary-Lou's red towel so that sand and water go all over Britt. She sits up with a jerk and rips off her sunglasses.

'Adam!' she bawls.

But I don't give a damn about Britt Börjesson. I run into the water again and hurl the red towel as far as I can out into the lake.

'Oh, no! How could you, Adam!' shouts Mary-Lou.

There were white horses on the lake when I woke up. I stood at the window watching the waves crash relentlessly against the stone foundations of the jetty.

There was no question of taking the boat out in this wind. At least not just with oars. I could see it was a north-westerly.

I shrugged my shoulders. The net would have to wait. The lake was renowned for blowing up without warning, but it usually died down again just as quickly.

I made the tea and a couple of shrimp-paste sandwiches. As I ate I doodled absent-mindedly on the sketchpad in front of me. It was my view from the window: the jetty with the rocking boat, the spume, a herring gull winging its way in across the lake. I covered a whole sheet with small pencil sketches.

I pulled on my sweater and went out to the hens. The grass was soaking wet and my jeans turned dark a good way up the legs.

'Good morning,' I said as I opened the back doors of the old Volvo Duett. Siv shook herself and came to the doorway. I thought they were starting to get used to me

29

already. I gave her some corn and a little boiled rice that was left over from yesterday's dinner.

She threw herself enthusiastically on the rice.

'Grub's up, come on,' I cooed, peering into the car for Ruth. She was nowhere to be seen but I heard a faint clucking sound from further inside. I went round and opened the front door and looked for her at the same time as checking for eggs. There was no sign of either.

'Come on, Ruth,' I called soothingly and then stood and listened. I thought I could hear something from the back seat. I leant into the car and carefully raised the long seat cushion. There she was, sitting and straining. She looked at me uneasily, as if in doubt about whether she dare stay there. Finally she sprang up and scuttled out to join Siv at the rice.

I stared at the place where she'd been. There was a hollow filled with brown stuffing from the seats. There were two eggs in the nest. I picked them up and wiggled the seat back into position with one hand.

19°, scattered clouds, fresh north-westerly. Two eggs, I wrote that evening.

The lake was still choppy.

Mary-Lou is sailing across the bay. There's a strong wind and her Finn-class dinghy is dipping out of sight between the waves. I'm following it from my window with binoculars and it looks as if her sail is skimming the water.

When she ties up at the jetty her face breaks into a broad grin at my anxiety.

'It's wonderful when the wind's really fresh, Adam. You feel so alive.'

We walk through the woods to the meadow on the other side of the point. There are dog-roses and juniper bushes growing there, but above all flowers. Masses of them: saxifrage, cat's-foot, milkwort, oxeye daisies. Later in the summer there'll be meadow-sweet, yellow bedstraw and harebells. My dad and I have made a proper inventory. We've found seventy-four species and listed them by their Swedish and Latin names.

There are also some Bronze Age mounds on the meadow, giant cairns. After that it slopes steeply down to Lake Vättern. Mary-Lou has christened the whole meadow Bronze Age.

It's the first time I've sketched outdoors and I feel self-conscious when I go to the side of the house and sit down and try to draw a pink dog-rose that's just coming into bloom.

Mary-Lou is leaping around on the Bronze Age mounds. She likes grubbing about there, turning over the stones and peeking down into the hollows and crevices. I don't know what she's searching for. I don't think she knows herself, either.

'I want to make a discovery, Adam,' she shouts. 'I want to find something that no one else has found. Something that's thousands of years old.'

Every now and again she comes careering over to look at my drawing.

'You'll be an artist when you grow up,' she says.

'You'll be an explorer,' I reply.

But she has already gone. Swishing through the grassy meadow as fast as the summer breeze.

'Come and see, Adam! There's a bird's nest here with four chicks in,' she cries, half-hidden in a juniper bush.

Then we're sitting at the top of the slope gazing out across the lake. The waves are hardly noticeable from up here. We can't see a single boat despite having a view over such a huge expanse.

'I wonder how it was in the Bronze Age,' says Mary-Lou.'

'Maybe exactly the same as it is now,' I venture. 'A Bronze Age boy and a Bronze Age girl could have sat here once upon a time.'

'Imagine if we'd been here then. Just for a day. I'm going to be an archaeologist when I grow up and come back and excavate these graves.'

'There's nothing there, Mary-Lou. They've been investigated already.'

'That's what they think!'

I laugh. Ease myself a little further up the slope.

'You feeling okay?'

I nod my head.

'No problem.'

'How high do you think we are?'

I look down at the stony beach. See some terns flying past far below.

'Fifty metres, at least.'

I'm lying on my back on the grass looking up at the blue sky. After a while I can sense that Mary-Lou is doing the same. Something is happening to us as we lie there. Something I can't explain. A blade of grass is tickling my cheek and I squint up at Mary-Lou who is leaning over me.

'Are you ticklish?' she asks.

I shake my head.

She moves the blade of grass and tries it under my chin.

'No, stop,' I laugh.

'You're fibbing!'

We roll over several times on the grass. I try to take the blade of grass away from her. In the end she's right on top of me. Staring into my eyes. And I'm looking into hers, the only eyes I've ever seen that can simultaneously laugh and remain serious. And although we know each other, it's now that we first really see each other. Time stands still. Or it doesn't. Perhaps there's a short-circuit between the present and the Bronze Age. We're not the same people we were a minute ago. Well, we are the same. But there's something new between us. I feel a desire to touch her. I run my fingertips over her cheeks, over her dimples and lips. I don't know why I'm doing it.

'I want us always to be together,' I say. 'Will you promise, Mary-Lou?'

She laughs. Nods.

'Of course. Always, Adam.'

I tear out my drawing of the dog-rose from the sketchpad and write 'To Mary-Lou' at the bottom. I give it to her. She studies it intently. Then she looks up at me.

'Draw me, Adam!'

But I shake my head.

'I can't, Mary-Lou. I'll have to learn a lot more first. Then I'll do it. I promise. I'll draw you one day.'

'One day you'll be famous,' she says.

A few weeks later there's a barbecue in Mary-Lou's garden. There are lots of people and tables have been laid in a rectangular red-striped marquee because the weather forecast was for several days of low pressure. One of the old sow's piglets is rotating silently over a bed of glowing coals.

The man supervising the pig has been sitting in the garden since ten in the morning with only cans of beer for company. At some stage during the course of the day he must have failed in his duties, because when the time is up and Björn carves off a few slices to test, it turns out that the piglet is completely raw inside. It'll still be hours before it can be eaten.

Perhaps that's why everything goes wrong.

Björn just laughs. He brings out a selection of spirits on a trolley and exhorts the guests to have another pre-prandial drink. He pours out vodka and whisky and gin. Mary-Lou says it's all home-brew mixed with flavourings that he gets on mail order. He keeps the spirit in five-litre drums behind the threshing machine in the barn.

The atmosphere in the garden is getting rowdier. Britt Börjesson's raucous shrieks of mirth pierce great wounds in the summer evening. She's wearing a very low-cut dress that scarcely covers her breasts.

'She could well be the piglet's mother,' I murmur as Britt leans over the drinks table and almost lets one of her tits fall out on Björn.

Mary-Lou giggles so much that she nearly chokes and I have to slap her on the back.

'Why does your father bring her here every year?' she asks.

'I don't know,' I lie. 'They're workmates. She's an editor on the newspaper and revises Dad's articles. They've worked together for nearly twenty years.'

'But that doesn't mean they have to live together?'

'They don't. Only in the summer.'

But actually Britt owns half of our cottage, because she helped my dad financially when things were rather tight just after the divorce. Without Britt's money he wouldn't have been able to afford to keep it. That's why we have to have her here. It's her house too. But I don't say that. I'd rather die than tell Mary-Lou that.

By the time the pig is edible it's a rather drunken crowd who take their seats in the marquee. Bottles of red wine and cans of beer make their way down the table. Mary-Lou's mother, whose name is Irja, serves schnapps to those who want it. She's as deft as a professional waitress and is wearing a long yellow summer frock. She flutters between guests like a butterfly. Serving and conversing. It's pretty obvious she's accustomed to dealing with people. She's Director of Studies at a college in Stockholm and commutes between Norden Farm and the city in a midnight-blue VW Golf.

Irja sits with me and Mary-Lou for a few moments. She drinks almost nothing herself. What opportunity would she have? Her heels clatter like woodpecker beaks on the black stone slabs whenever she goes into the house to fetch something.

Mary-Lou and I gulp down our food and then wander along to the lake. It's a really fine evening and we take her boat out and trail lines for fish. We row back and forth across the bay between the northern peninsula and our own. The lake is as smooth as glass. House-martins swoop around the boat, skimming the surface for insects.

'It's going to rain tonight,' says Mary-Lou. 'That's why the fish aren't biting.'

On our fourth or fifth crossing we notice the wind freshening up. I'm in a hurry to get back to the jetty. The waves are already high by the time we come in.

'This lake is crazy,' I say as we're tying up. I can feel my knees trembling.

'It certainly can blow up fast,' she says tranquilly.

She knows. She's lived by the lake the whole of her twelve-year-old life. She's not like me: a summer visitor, an outsider.

When we come up to the garden we find the party has entered a new phase. The suckling pig is finished and people have dispersed in smaller groups. Some are still in the marquee drinking coffee. I can see my father chatting on his eternal mobile phone under one of the fruit trees. He's holding an amber drink in one hand and beckons with it as we approach. We go over to him.

'Who were you talking to?'

'Örjan on the paper. He might come out for a few days.'

'Where's Britt?' I ask.

'No idea,' Dad says, looking around.

Mary-Lou and I take our drinks and go in to see what's on TV. It's quiet and peaceful inside. As I slip off to the loo I hear a noise from a room I know is Björn's study. My first thought is that it might be a burglar. I stand outside the door and listen. There's a rustling sound. A voice whispering something I can't make out. A groan.

I realise it can't be a burglar, but as I'm about to continue on my way to the toilet Mary-Lou's mother appears from nowhere. She asks why I'm standing there in the dark. I shrug my shoulders. Maybe I also cast a sidelong glance at the door. Or maybe she hears it herself. Because in the next instant she has grasped the handle, opened the door and switched on the light.

Björn's bald red pate pops up from the black leather sofa opposite the desk. He only has an unbuttoned white shirt on. The rest of his clothes are strewn all over the floor. He gapes at the door in astonishment. As if only now does it strike him that he should have locked it. From the sofa comes a shrill voice:

'What is it, darling?'

It's the voice I know better than anyone else's: Britt Börjesson's.

I've thought about the days that followed many times and I think I can give an account of most of what

37

happened. But there's nothing that even hints at what that banal event on the leather sofa might lead to. No one could have foreseen it. I don't notice anything. My father is usually very observant, but in this instance is something of an enigma.

The one who takes it best is probably Mary-Lou's mother, who seems to view it all quite objectively. She is calm and sensible; she carries on being the same brisk and elegant Irja as before. Her thick hair is cut in a modern medium-length style and every time she turns her head all her hair moves too. She turns her head a lot during the next few days. Those are the kind of meaningless details I recall. They're razor-sharp in my memory.

Björn looks as guilty as a dog caught with a lambchop in its jaws. He goes on apologising for days on end. Insists that it will never happen again.

Dad merely shakes his head at everything.

'It's so bloody typical of BB,' he says.

At my father's instigation Britt goes home to Stockholm for a while. I almost feel a bit sorry for her. She suddenly looks so lost and lonely. And although I'm really fed up with her constant presence in the house, I ought perhaps to correct the picture of her that I've given. She's not entirely like that. It's my subjective portrait. I'm highlighting the worst aspects of her.

Britt is a real workaholic. Long before Dad and I are awake in the mornings she'll have her jeans and shirt on and be whistling away somewhere. She'll be painting the house, replacing broken roof tiles, wallpapering the living-room, installing air vents in the larder, putting new roofing felt on the privy. Her carrot-red hair will be gathered on top of her head and held in place by a white cotton ribbon hanging down in front. When I was little I thought she looked like an American Indian.

Dad has never been very practical. He mows the grass. Occasionally, anyway. That's his summer job. And the chicken coop is partly his doing, too. When the fox paid its second visit, Björn suggested that we borrow his old mothballed Volvo Duett to put the chickens in at night. It was only standing gathering dust. My father leapt at the offer. He seemed to think it was a splendid notion. So one Sunday afternoon Björn drove the car right into the chicken run. And there it's been ever since.

Dad regards the cottage as his sanctuary. He comes here to relax from the stress of the newspaper, to keep his old interest in botany going and to write a few pages of his never-ending novel.

Without Britt the cottage would slowly and surely have crumbled into ruin. I can also see that she can't be blamed for everything that happened. For what she did herself, of course. For that disgraceful session with Björn. But beyond that? I know she took it very hard. But that doesn't alter my opinion of her: I don't like her.

I can never understand why Mary-Lou hides what she feels. She puts on a nonchalant air and talks about it in a bantering kind of way. She says it's just about what you could expect of a pig feast. It's as if it doesn't bother her in the slightest.

But the truth is that the event devastates her life like a bombshell. For her it's the worst thing that could have happened. Everything she believes in is smashed to smithereens. Her father betrays her mother with another woman in their own home.

I think Mary-Lou loses her sense of proportion over it. It's magnified for her. It gnaws into her brain and clouds her vision. It's a perfectly natural reaction for a twelve-year-old. I would probably have reacted the same way myself. Childhood is at best an innocent tale of a king and a queen. Sooner or later you see through it all. You come to see that your parents are just normal people with the same faults and weaknesses as everyone else. But the discovery is a complete shock for Mary-Lou.

It's a pity she manages to hide it so skilfully. There's nothing to indicate the crisis she's going through.

Well, perhaps one thing: the spontaneous curiosity that I like in her becomes more forced. It's as if she's trying to seek out exciting situations to show me she's quite indifferent to what's happened.

I hear the siren miles away. I'm in the garden trying to mend a puncture in my bike. My dad has got up from his computer and come out on to the steps.

The sound is faint at first and we can hear it only intermittently, as if the wind keeps catching it and sweeping it down to the lake. Then it gets more distinct. It puts me in mind of a howling wolf roaming through the countryside. Running to and fro roaring out its pain and sorrow.

I try to follow the vehicle's route along the twisting road. Imagine I can hear it braking for the sharp bend at the bus shelter, speeding up on the straight stretch past the fields, turning off before the point and heading west.

When the noise suddenly ceases everything is quiet. My father has come over on to the lawn and is standing beside me.

I know exactly where the ambulance has stopped. I can tell that he knows too.

Dad rings the hospital that afternoon. He talks to Irja for a long time. I'm right next to him listening and understanding.

Mary-Lou's life is not in danger. She's conscious but has injured her spine. Some vertebrae have been crushed. There's nothing more they can say at present.

She had jumped down from the cherry tree and landed on the black granite slabs below.

She had waited nine days before she did it.

By morning the waves had subsided: they were just ripples on the surface. When I went outside I could hear a monotonous growl from across the bay and could make out a tractor chugging up and down a field. From here it looked like a fly. Björn was haymaking. I took it as a sign that more stable weather was coming.

I ate two sandwiches of eggs fried both sides and drank my tea on the jetty. The tractor fell silent. The wagtail came purling through the air and settled on the end of the jetty twitching its tail feathers. I wanted to try and draw it and rummaged through the new pencils I'd bought. I chose a 2B and the soft lead seemed to melt into the paper as I filled in its body: its little head with the white cheek and watchful dark eyes, the black bib on its breast, the proud tail, its nimble matchstick legs.

Just as I'd finished and was turning the sheet it flew ashore. I saw it disappear under a tile on the roof right up by the chimney.

I stayed where I was for a few minutes and kept my eye on the spot.

All that could be heard were the tiny waves lapping the shingle at the water's edge. They were real summer waves. I closed my eyes and let my body fill up with the constant rippling. This must be an ancient sound, I thought. This is how the Earth must have sounded at the beginning of time. In the Bronze Age. And even earlier: before mankind existed.

After Mary-Lou's accident Norden Farm collapses like a house of cards. She'd made us all see the event on the leather sofa from a different point of view. Mary-Lou's.

I don't know whether it's the right decision or not but Irja is talking to my father about leaving Björn. For Mary-Lou's sake. She says she's contemplating moving to Stockholm.

Björn is starting to drink. He was no paragon before, but alcohol didn't seem to affect him. Not the way it does others. He had an almost uncanny ability to cope with all the work on the farm single-handed. He could empty the nets first thing in the morning and drive the catch to town. Weld a rusting Volvo together before lunch. Thresh the wheat in the afternoon. Drive the tractor to Odal with two trailers to deliver the corn, sort out some complicated deal on the industrial estate and return home in the evening with the trailers full of drainage pipes for the clover bank by the lake and garden furniture for a new seating area he was planning. Then he would hop on the tractor again and plough till long gone midnight. After which he would wind down by working on the rusty Volvo before dropping into bed. That's how he went on. Day after day.

No one understood how he managed. But Björn himself would just laugh and wipe some beads of sweat off his brow. He scurried around fast, bent forward at an angle, as if on the point of falling headlong. His feet hardly left the ground. He always looked as if he was skiing. He was really speedy.

But now it's as if something's broken in him. The incredible flow of energy that held his twenty-hour days together, that made his life function, perhaps his love for Irja or Mary-Lou, fails him.

He tries to get down to work as before. But he starts forgetting things. A hay-press is left out in a field for several weeks. He flits from one task to another without finishing anything properly. He might attach the harrow and drive out of the yard, suddenly jump off the tractor and start painting the workshop, and then do nothing for

43

*a while or sit down and have a drink with a summer
visitor who's come to buy some char.*

And he's stopped laughing.

When I rowed out to take in the net I had trouble
locating it. It wasn't where I thought it should be and it
occurred to me that the strong wind might have driven it
offshore. Then I saw one of the red plastic floats a little
further out on the lake.

They say fishing is difficult in Lake Vättern. It's true
that it's a very big lake. It gets deep suddenly, and the
water is crystal clear. You have to know where the fish
are, exactly where they are, or you don't get any. Dad and
I knew quite a lot about that. Not getting any, I mean. But
there were fish there all right. Salmon, whitefish,
grayling, pike and perch – and char, of course. We'd
caught whitefish a number of times and one summer we
caught a bream that weighed nearly three kilos.

But there were none of them in the net I hauled up
that morning. It was empty. I felt totally indecisive, the
way I am sometimes, and couldn't make up my mind
whether to leave the net where it was or move it or take
it out for good. I think I sat there in the boat for about
a quarter of an hour wondering what to do. It made me
really break out into a sweat. In the end I left it where
it was.

*I visit Mary-Lou in hospital a week after the accident. My
dad is with me and we bring her a box of chocolates and
a bunch of flowers that I've picked in the meadow on the*

other side of the woods. Mostly harebells, because I know
she likes them.

It's one of the hottest days of summer and the city is
empty. A few individuals can be glimpsed on park
benches in the deepest shade. The hospital is so quiet
that it almost seems abandoned. The entrance doors
are ajar, the corridors deserted. A curtain is wafting
indolently in a coffee lounge. Not a nurse in sight. We
slide along on the polished floor of Ward 4 and
eventually find room 21 at the far end of a corridor.

Mary-Lou is expecting us and doesn't stir when we
push open the door. She's lying on her back in a big
tubular steel bed by the window. There are two vases of
flowers on her bedside table. Her face is pale and she
looks smaller to me than before.

'Hello, Mary-Lou,' my father says.

She inclines her head almost imperceptibly in reply.

'How are you?' I ask.

'Okay,' she says.

'It's as hot as hell outside,' I go on, making a grimace,
mainly because I can't think of anything else to say. And
maybe partly because I want to tell her there's some
advantage at least in being in this cool room.

She says nothing.

'Your mum and dad send their love,' my father says.

Though it's pretty superfluous since Irja visits every
day.

I look around the room. It's quite small, about the
same size as mine at home. There's a little lobby with a
toilet at the entrance. I think it's nice for her to be on her

45

own. You need a room of your own if you're having to lie in a special bed for several weeks.

'What a good view you've got,' my father says, indicating the leafy park.

Mary-Lou still doesn't say anything.

Then Dad finally thinks to take the chocolates out of their bag and I hand over the flowers I've been holding behind my back. Her face lights up when she sees the harebells. Fleetingly, like the sun glinting out from behind a grey cloud.

'Thanks,' she says. 'They're lovely.'

'They're from the Bronze Age,' I say. 'There are lots there now.'

I say that because I want her to know that these flowers mean more than ordinary flowers. They're from our meadow. I can see she has tears in her eyes.

'We'll go there when you get out.'

Mary-Lou nods. She swallows. Then she looks at me with eyes that are quite different from what I'm used to. Her look startles me. She says, 'I may never be able to do it, Adam. I may have to stay here for ever.'

I squirm, unsure what to say. I think I'm close to bursting into tears. I know it's a serious injury to her spine. That it'll take a long time for her to recover. That she may never be completely right again. But she was lucky too. The injury is low down. She landed on her backside. That's probably why she's still alive.

I think all that before I have the shock of seeing her eyes. I can hear my father talking as if far away about the great progress medical science is making. But I'm

46

not listening. I'm just staring at Mary-Lou. Her eyes are completely empty. It's like looking into two black holes. Mary-Lou isn't there.

I visit her again. She's tired and low. She barely responds when we speak to her and after a while she starts crying. A young nurse with dark hair in a pigtail comes in and says it would be best if Mary-Lou rested now.

A few days later we go back to Stockholm. Dad's holiday is over.

When we return the following summer Mary-Lou and Irja have left. Björn is living alone at Norden Farm and fighting an unequal battle against weeds and home-brewed spirits.

The summer Mary-Lou will be thirteen is the first time there won't be a party in the big garden.

On her birthday I go to the Bronze Age and pick a bunch of flowers and put them on one of the cairns of stones. I stand in silence for a moment, praying for Mary-Lou to get better and for things to be as they were.

We only stay for a few days. I think both my dad and I feel the same. That it's not right to be here. He goes out there again later on. Sometimes on his own. Once with Britt. But I don't go. I can't. I can't put it behind me. It's as if I fell myself. My father said afterwards that I made too much of everything. Possibly. But it didn't feel like it at the time.

Dad phones Irja occasionally. She says the situation is unchanged and that she's worried about Mary-Lou. She's become introverted and bitter. I almost think Dad's *quite interested in Irja. That something might be developing between them. I mean, why not? It would fit the general pattern. But nothing ever comes of it. Dad's too lazy. He can't make the effort to commit himself. He thinks he's okay as he is. He's got me, after all.*

I shook my head and stared out across the lake, towards Norden Farm. Life is so fragile, I thought. It can change as fast as you can swat a mosquito. Tomorrow or in five minutes' time everything can look quite different.

Is there any meaning to events, or in the meaningless things that happen to us as individuals? A couple of cold-callers from some religious sect came knocking on our door last winter and talked about that. They were skinny blokes in suits and glasses with black hair combed straight back. I intended getting rid of them pretty swiftly but they had the knack of turning every-thing I said into absorbing questions that they could go on to answer. They said of course there was. That there was a meaning to everything that happened. That our task in life was to discover the meaning.

I nodded agreement. Said it was something to think about. I did that because I could see it was the only way to make them go. But there was one question burning on my lips the whole time: If a twelve-year-old girl jumps from the top of her cherry tree and cripples herself, what's the meaning of that?

I never said it. I nodded and agreed with everything. It was cowardly, but I am a coward sometimes.

I gradually realised that there were conflicting

interpretations of Mary-Lou's leap from the tree. To me it was crystal clear. She was trying to take her own life. But I could see that Björn and Irja thought she had fallen. That it was an accident! Even my dad, who's meant to be a critical journalist, seemed more disposed towards the accident theory. Are adults blind? Or is it that they can't deal with unpalatable truths?

My feelings about it were quite different. It may sound odd, but I secretly admired Mary-Lou for what she'd done. I was impressed by her courage, by her resolute determination. When I thought about it my whole body quivered. It was so typically Mary-Lou. She always followed her feelings. That's what she was like.

I cycled to the supermarket that afternoon. I stopped off at the bus shelter on the main road and felt in our roadside letter box. There was a postcard from Damascus. My dad was finding it tough because it was so hot, he wrote. Nearly forty degrees in the shade.

As I pedalled on I could see acres of mayweed, like frilly priest's collars, giving the wheat fields a covering of white froth. The air was dry. It was hot here too. There was a heavy scent of ripening corn. I was sweating even though I was cycling slowly. Forty degrees in the shade. Poor old Dad!

I bought bread and milk and buttermilk and an expensive tube of meat paste. Then I went and rang my mother. She sounded pleased when she heard it was me. I said everything was absolutely fine. That the sun was shining and that I'd got really brown.

When we'd said goodbye and take care of yourself and phone again soon, I took out the gold visiting card and keyed in the seven-digit number. I counted the rings at the other end. She answered in the middle of the fourth.

'Hello. Mary-Lou Arvnell.'

'Hi . . . This is Adam.'

There was silence on the line for a few seconds. I thought I could hear her draw in her breath.

'Hi.'

'I promised I'd ring.'

'Yes, I'm glad you have.'

'How are things in the city?'

'Hot!'

'Here too. Even in the water!'

'Are you phoning from the shop?'

'Yes. I could hardly make it here on the bike.'

'I can imagine.'

I thought her voice sounded quite cheerful. At any rate happier than I'd expected. Or was it just an act?

'I met Björn the other day. He came over to say hello.'

'Oh.'

This was obviously a sensitive issue, so I tried to think of a way to change the subject.

'I've been drawing flowers up at the Bronze Age. It's really nice there at the moment.'

'Oh.'

I screwed up my courage. Watched a dark-blue Golf turn in and park at the supermarket. But saw it had German number plates. Finally asked, 'Have you thought any more about what we discussed?'

Another momentary silence.

'Coming out, you mean?'

'Yeah. It would be brilliant if you could.'

'Mummy and I have talked it over. She thinks it's a good idea. She'd like me to.'

'So would I,' I interjected eagerly. 'You can sleep in Britt's room. That's the best in the whole house.'

Silence at the other end again.

Then Mary-Lou said, 'I think I will, Adam. I think I'll come!'

Back at the cottage, I had no idea how I'd got there. Half an hour of my life had gone missing. I'd cycled four miles without being conscious of it. I'd been somewhere else entirely. I suppose I should have been thankful that I hadn't been knocked down, because I must have passed the bus heading in the opposite direction.

When I put Siv and Ruth to bed that night I was still feeling elated. The back seat was empty. I told them they'd better pull their socks up. I explained that we were expecting a visitor.

'Cluck, cluck, cluck,' they said, waggling their heads in concern.

I trotted round with the brush and dustpan and swept up two dead bumblebees from under the window in the living room. I threw them and a little bit of dirt out of the open door, and wondered whether to shake out the rag-rug in the kitchen, but decided it didn't need it. It had only been me here.

I went in the garden and cut some sprays of jasmine and put them in a slender ceramic vase on the window-sill in Britt's room. And got out the old china pot that Britt had bought at an auction.

27°, sunny, light southerly breeze, I wrote in my diary.

I had trouble getting to sleep. I could hear the wind in the trees and I kept wondering if the lake would freshen up again. There was a fast throbbing audible under the blanket. It was my fishing-boat heart beginning to pound.

Steady, little heart.

Mary-Lou is coming. Everything will be all right.

2

'Sure you don't want any?'

'Yes.'

Mary-Lou was sitting on the jetty staring out across the lake. She didn't look at me as she answered. The evening sun caressed her cheek and lit up her dark brown hair with a halo. I went over and sat down cross-legged by her side. I blew cautiously on the hot tea.

'It's really lovely,' she said.

'I'm glad you came.'

She turned her head at last, giving me a brief glance. I met her eyes, her empty eyes, and felt another stab in my heart. Oh God, I thought. Oh God, what have you done to Mary-Lou? Then she looked away again.

We sat in silence. Let the evening speak. Against the vague murmur of the waves, a fibreglass speedboat rounded the point, ripping up the smooth water as it headed in to Norrängen, and despite its distance out on the lake we could hear what they were saying on board as clearly as if they'd been sitting in the boat here at the jetty. Every word carried.

When it had gone we could even hear Siv and Ruth muttering about something over in the chicken run.

'It's fab that you've got chickens,' said Mary-Lou.

I agreed. 'Even though they're not laying eggs.'

'Maybe they're moulting,' she suggested.

'What d'you mean?'

'They lose their feathers. It takes a few weeks for the new ones to grow.'

I thought about it. Ruth and Siv might simply be feeling a bit out of sorts, of course.

'Would you like to see?' I asked, handing her the sketchpad.

I wanted her to know how differently I drew nowadays. That I'd learnt something in the last three years.

She nodded and took the pad and flicked quickly through it.

'They're good,' she said, handing it back.

'How's your singing coming on?'

She sat in silence. It didn't seem as if she was intending to respond. I tried to ease the conversation along.

'I was just thinking about when we ran into each other in Stockholm. You were on your way to sing in St Sophia's Church.'

'Oh, yes.'

'Is that what you're going to go in for, singing?'

She didn't reply immediately. When she did speak, it was in a voice so cold that it made me shiver.

'What do you think I'm going to be, Adam? Isn't it obvious? A bloody care package, that's what I'm going to be!'

She wheeled round hard and fast and swept back on to land, losing momentum as soon as she hit the lawn. She came to a halt at the foot of the steps by the door and yelled at the top of her voice, 'Can't you come and help me for Christ's sake!'

When she had shut herself in Britt's room I sat for a while at the table by the window. I drew without thinking about what I was doing. My hand could look after itself. Later on I got up and went to the jetty to brush my teeth. When I came back I paused outside her door to ask whether she needed any assistance. There was no response. Perhaps she had gone to sleep.

'I'm going to bed now, Mary-Lou. If there's anything you want, just call.'

I jotted a line in my diary: *22°, sunny, light southerly breeze. Mary-Lou here.*

I snuggled into bed, tried to read for a bit but couldn't concentrate. I turned off the light and lay awake for ages.

I woke up early, filled the pan ready for tea, trying to move about quietly, and crept out to water the willow-herb. It was a fine day. The summer was shaping up. A yacht that had put into the bay for the night was gliding out with flapping mainsail, and two diminutive figures in the cockpit were waving to me. Their lifejackets were up over their ears and I could only see their blond hair sticking out. I waved back, and strolled over to the chicken run. There were a lot of feathers on the ground and I thought Mary-Lou might be right, Ruth and Siv must be moulting.

When I came in again the water was boiling. I turned off the stove, put in a tea bag, cut the bread and laid the table. Fetched the tube of meat paste from the larder. I heard sounds from Mary-Lou's room. The door opened and she came into view. Pushing with her arms, she grimaced slightly as she juddered over the threshold and rolled into the kitchen.

'I'll get rid of that sill,' I said.

'Have you still not got an inside loo?'

I shook my head.

'Only the outside privy.'

The privy was a red hut up the hill on the edge of the woods, well away from the house. A semi-paved path led up to it. There was a view of the entire bay through the gaps in the door.

'And how do you think I'm going to get there?'

I realised we had a problem. I hadn't given any thought to such complications. Getting up to the privy in a wheelchair would scarcely be possible at all. Not even with me pushing her. Then I remembered my dad sometimes used to push me there in the wheelbarrow when I was little. It was great fun.

'Wait and see!'

I went out into the garden and eventually found the wheelbarrow behind the outhouse. Looking at it, it didn't seem any too clean. I got two plastic sacks from the outhouse and laid them in it. The blue and white sailor's cap that Dad had for his thirtieth birthday was on a nearby hook. I stuck it on my head. Then sped across the lawn with the barrow, parked it neatly in front of the door, went in and made a bow.

'Adam's Taxis, at your service.'

Mary-Lou didn't seem amused. She just leant forward and stretched her arms towards me. I took hold of her exactly like that, in my arms, so that her head and shoulders were over my shoulder, and carried her carefully out of the door. She was much lighter than I'd expected, like a shop-window mannequin, I thought, as I lowered her gently into the wheelbarrow with her legs dangling over one end.

'To the shithouse!' I cried, taking a firm grip on the wooden handles.

It was quite a bumpy ride, and the last bit I really had to take a run at, so the barrow's rubber wheel sort of bounced up the hill.

'Here we are, madam,' I said, setting down the barrow outside the red wooden hut. I opened the door wide for her.

'Stop it now,' she said, holding out her arms to be hoisted out.

I tried the same technique again, but didn't get her so high up. Our faces were on a level, her cheek touched mine for an instant, her body hung the length of mine. I stood her beside the barrow, then bent over a little, found a new grip and carried her in.

'I'll wait down there,' I said, nodding towards the lake.

She made no response. I closed the door on her and went and sat by the water. I waited for ages. In the end I began to wonder if she had gone to sleep in there. Just as I got up to go and check, she called me.

'There's a helluva lot of bees in here,' she cried, kicking the door open. Some bees came flying out with an angry buzz that faded as they disappeared into the woods.

'I think they must have a nest nearby,' I said.

'Get me out of here!' Mary-Lou shrieked, her arms outstretched again. I went up close and got a good hold, beginning to improve my method, and carried her to the barrow.

We jolted back down the stony hill. As I lifted her into the cottage, my concentration wavered a bit too soon and I almost hit her head on the doorway into the kitchen, realising it only at the last minute but successfully lowering her into the wheelchair again. I felt quite pleased with myself and considered I'd managed it all reasonably well.

'Would you like some breakfast?'

She nodded. But when I poured out the tea, she turned up her nose at it. I'd forgotten to fish out the tea bag and the result was a thick dark brown liquid.

'I'll make some fresh,' I said, chucking it away down the sink. 'Just have a sandwich for now.'

'Isn't there any coffee?'

'Would you rather have that?'

Another nod.

I hunted through the cupboard, shook my head.

'I'll buy some.'

'You haven't got any butter, either?'

I shook my head again.

'I didn't think we'd need it if we had cheese spread.'

The second brew was more successful and I poured some out for Mary-Lou. Then I made a sandwich of meat paste. She sipped her tea. I asked whether she wouldn't like a sandwich anyway.

'You ought to eat something. There are some tins of peaches. They're good.'

'I'm not hungry.'

I made another sandwich. Pointed to a boat sailing past. Mary-Lou ignored it. I fetched my book on perspective drawing and read that while I ate.

'Say if you want any more tea.'

'No thanks.'

'What would you like to do?'

'Nothing in particular.'

'I thought we could go to the Bronze Age.'

'I'd rather stay here.'

'Okay. That's fine too.'

She stood up and I wheeled her chair out through the porch and down the steps on to the grass before going back in to carry her out.

'Do you have to hold me like a rag doll?'

'Sorry.'

We went and sat on the jetty. Mary-Lou in her chair, right at the end. She had a notepad in brown covers on her lap and was writing in it every now and again. After a while she looked up, out across the bay, over towards Norden Farm. She sat in silence for such long periods that I wondered whether she'd fallen asleep.

I was dying to draw her as she sat there with the whole bay behind her, but I wasn't sure whether she would like it if I drew her in secret, so I abandoned the idea. I sank into a kind of trance. Listening to the waves. Meditating.

I sat there for about a quarter of an hour, or it may

have been an hour, I don't know, just watching the dark green waves rolling into the bay and breaking in a frothy chuckle just before the beach. They were real bathing waves today, the sort we used to jump in when we were little. I was almost inclined to go in now.

When I raised my eyes I saw that Mary-Lou had swivelled her chair round and was looking at me.

'It's too hot. I want to go back to the house,' she said.

'I'll help you.'

I wheeled her up to the cottage, lifted her out and carried her into her room and sat her gently on the side of the bed. Then went and brought the wheelchair in.

'Can you close the door, please,' she said when I'd stood the chair by the bed.

'I think I'll cycle to the shop,' I said. 'Is there anything in particular you'd like?'

'No.'

'See you later, then.'

I shut the door, went out into the sunshine. I pushed my bike out through the gate and pedalled slowly along the wheel tracks in the meadow.

This isn't going to work, I thought. She's not functioning. She's a different person. We don't know one another.

I began to think it might be best if I rang the taxi service and asked them to come and collect her.

When I got back she was sitting at the table by the window reading my weather journal. She laid it down when I came in with a bulging paper carrier bag from the supermarket that I heaved up on to the kitchen worktop.

'Hi,' I said.

She didn't respond.

'I've bought tomatoes and cucumber and lettuce. And coffee,' I added, starting to unpack everything. I folded up the bag and placed it on the pile of newspapers under the bookshelves and put the food away in the larder.

'What would you like for lunch?' I called. 'I could eat a horse.'

'What is there?'

I looked around.

'Stacks of things. Come and see.'

I heard her turn the wheelchair and jolt over the threshold. She inspected the deep wooden shelves full of tins. There must have been at least a hundred. Haricot beans, red beans, pea soup, minced meat and potato hash, stew, tuna, fishballs, sardines, marinated herring, meatballs, tomatoes, peas, sweetcorn, asparagus, new potatoes and a whole shelf of nothing but tinned fruit.

'It's my dad's stores,' I said. 'He comes here to work sometimes.'

'What do you usually eat?' Mary-Lou asked.

'It varies. I can make my dad's special if you like.'

'What's that?'

I picked out a tin of haricot beans and one of fishballs in lobster sauce.

'You mix these together, add a drop of oil and a pinch of salt and black pepper. It's very tasty.'

'Yuck,' she said. 'Are tins all you've got?'

I thought it might be best not to tell her what my father did when he was here writing in the autumn and lined up tins in rows on the stove. So they're nice and warm when you want them.

'And there's pasta and instant potato and rice and stuff in the kitchen cupboard.'

'I'm not hungry.'

'You've got to eat, Mary-Lou.'

'Can you make a tomato salad?'

'No problem.'

I whistled as I prepared the food. Sliced three firm tomatoes and half a cucumber and arranged it all on a thick bed of lettuce leaves. I thought there ought to be some slivers of onion on top but I'd forgotten to buy any. I went out to the larder and got a jar of black olives and added a dozen to the salad. I made a dressing of oil and a few drops of juice from a plastic lemon, stirred in a little mustard plus salt and pepper. Cut some French bread that I'd bought. It was so fresh that it still smelt.

I laid the table with plates and glasses. Mary-Lou's eyes followed my every move.

'Do you do all the cooking?'

I nodded as I rinsed my hands under the tap.

'Dad's hardly ever at home. You can't eat pizza day after day. What would you like to drink, milk or water?'

'Water.'

I poured out a glass of water for her and got the milk carton from the fridge. We ate in silence. The salad was actually pretty good. I dipped my bread in the dressing that collected on the plate. Mary-Lou just picked at her food. She put the olives to one side. She didn't want any dressing. She took a slice of bread only unwillingly, nibbled at it and then left it on the plate, which she pushed away, saying she was completely full.

I banged the plates down as I cleared the table. I dumped her food in the scrap pail for the chickens and slammed the door of the cupboard under the sink.

'Siv and Ruth will be over the moon,' I said. 'They love salad.'

I went out into the garden. I needed some fresh air. Mary-Lou wanted to stay inside. Fine, I thought. She can sit in there and rot. I stood on the lawn, uncertain where to go, just feeling I wanted to get away.

I wandered aimlessly along the lakeshore for several hours. I eventually found myself up by the big rocks at the end of the point. I sat down to think. I was beginning to feel a bit better.

There was a note on the kitchen table when I got back: *I've gone to bed. Please don't wake me. Mary-Lou.*

I looked at the clock. It was five to six. I screwed up the note and slung it in the bin. I noticed that she had banished the vase of jasmine to the kitchen worktop.

I went outside to talk about feathers with Siv and Ruth.

'Shall we take the boat out?'
Mary-Lou shook her head.
'Do you want to go for a dip?'
Another shake of the head, almost imperceptible.
'Shall we go for a walk in the enchanted forest?'

She didn't even shake her head this time, just stared straight in front of her.

'No,' she said eventually, 'I don't feel like it.'

'What do you feel like, then?'

Another pause.

'Nothing, Adam. Nothing in particular. Do what you want yourself, but don't bother about me. Okay?'

Short pause.

'No. It's not okay. If you're going to be here we should be together. Otherwise you might as well go home.'

Mary-Lou said nothing.

'What's wrong?'

She still didn't reply.

'Is it me?'

She shook her head once more.

'Is it all too difficult?'

Now not even a shake of the head, just her fixed gaze.

'Is that it, Mary-Lou? Is coming back here too much for you? If so, tell me. I can see it's hard. I can, really.'

She spun her wheelchair round so violently that it nearly tipped over. She directed her eyes, her black mournful eyes, at me. They tugged at my heart yet again.

'For God's sake cut it out, Adam! Stop feeling sorry for me! They'll look after me. That's what people pay for. Society can deal with this package. They'll come and fetch it when I ring.'

She swallowed a lump in her throat, dried her lips on her hand, and continued her outburst: 'I don't give a shit about your bloody cottage or Norden Farm! It means sod all to me! Do you hear? Sod all!'

Silence. I was thinking frantically, feeling my patience at an end. I'd had enough. As slowly and emphatically as I could, I said, 'I don't feel sorry for you, Mary-Lou. It's you yourself who do. You're the most spoilt girl I've ever met.'

Complete silence. I was beside myself with rage. Mary-Lou said nothing. Just stared out over the water.

I knew I had to work off my anger somehow. I turned on my heel and stomped back to the cottage, shouting over my shoulder, 'I'm going for a swim!'

I went indoors, snatched up my trunks and put them on. By the time I came out my fury had really taken hold, spreading through me like wildfire. I saw Mary-Lou sitting in her wheelchair under the alder trees by the beach and before I knew what had come over me I was charging at full speed down to the shore, grabbing the wheelchair handles and running with it straight out into the water. The large wheels rolled easily over the shallow sandy bottom. I could feel the ribbed surface as a faint vibration through the handles. The water sprayed up around us. Mary-Lou sat as stiff as a poker, panic-stricken, gripping the armrests tight. Then she raised herself to a half-standing position, twisted her head round, lashed out at me with one arm as if I was some sort of vermin, and yelled up to the skies, 'Stop, you bloody idiot! Stop it! Adam, stop!'

I pushed even faster. High-stepping through the water as it rose around her, halfway up the wheelchair.

'I'm not going to stop!' I roared.

But in the end I couldn't get any further. The

wheelchair came to a halt. The water was up to her chest. She was no longer shouting at me. I flung myself headlong into the water, pretended to swim several metres beneath the surface and came up with a snort. I stood there, bent double, gasping with the effort.

She sat in the wheelchair without saying a word. Her clothes clung to her skin. Her hair was sopping. Water streamed down her face. I hardly dared look at her. The cold dip had also cooled my temper and I felt rather ashamed of myself. Yet at the same time I was beginning to see the funny side of the situation. I was afraid of bursting out laughing. I dived again and managed to splash my way over to the jetty. I climbed up over the stones and sat on the warm boards. The risk of laughter seemed to diminish with distance.

Mary-Lou had turned her wheelchair and started pushing towards the shore. She was making short powerful thrusts with her arms. The chair moved sluggishly through the water. She stopped when she got it up on to the beach and without looking at me called, 'If you've finished swimming you could come and help me in.'

It was teeming down with rain. Through the window I could see the raindrops sort of fused into long bright rods slicing through the air. I wondered if that was how the expression raining stair-rods had come about.

Mary-Lou was in her room, sitting in her chair reading. The door was open but it might as well have been closed. There was a wary silence between us. We

66

weren't speaking to each other unnecessarily. Or rather, Mary-Lou wasn't saying much.

I peered out again to see whether there was any sign of it easing off, but since it didn't look like it, I put my father's old leather jacket over my head and decided to brave it. I hesitated outside the door for a few seconds before shooting over to the outhouse. Pausing to get my breath back, I took a few handfuls of corn and went across to the chicken coop. As I opened the doors of the Volvo the leather jacket slipped off and I was left standing unprotected in the downpour. I slung the corn hastily into the car, rubbed my hands together to remove all the grain that had stuck to my wet skin, picked up the leather jacket from the ground and pulled it over me again.

'You'll have to stay in today,' I said, closing the doors on them.

I scuttled back to the outhouse and stood on the concrete floor shaking myself like a wet dog. Then I rooted around among the tools that Britt had arranged so neatly on the IKEA shelving by the window. I took a hammer, pliers, saw and a big screwdriver, and holding them close to my chest launched myself out again into the pouring rain. I could see Mary-Lou's face through the window as I zoomed past. She was watching me quite impassively. I couldn't be sure whether she registered me or was staring straight through me.

'What bloody awful weather!' I yelled as I yanked the door open and dived into the porch.

I put the tools on a chair and lay down on the floor to inspect my task more closely. It occurred to me now that

I knew nothing about door sills, why they existed, what the point of them was, how they were installed, and above all, how to take them out.

I'd thought perhaps I could saw it in line with the door frame and then knock it away with the hammer, but once down on a level with it I realised it must be fastened to the floor. Would I be able to prise it up with the claw hammer or would I need one of those small crowbars?

I didn't think Britt possessed such a thing so I decided to have a go with what I'd got.

'There'll be a bit of a racket now,' I called out.

I attacked the first threshold with a few blows of the hammer. The whole house reverberated, teacups rattled in the kitchen. The sill didn't budge, but got badly dented. I pondered for a moment and then hammered in the screwdriver between the sill and the floor. Heaving on the handle, I managed to get it about half a centimetre off the floor. Enough to ease the claw of the hammer into the gap and prise it up further. The nails groaned their reluctance as they loosened their grip. When the sill eventually freed itself I lost my balance and fell into the kitchen on my arse. I couldn't help laughing at myself.

Encouraged by this success, I moved on to the others. The larder door was child's play. By the time I got to Mary-Lou's door I was feeling pretty warm. I banged in the screwdriver in practised fashion and prised up both ends, inserted the hammer and lifted the sill carefully and confidently in one smooth operation. I wished she'd been watching.

'I'll fix up a ramp for the outside door later,' I said to her back as I stood with the sill in my hand.

Her back didn't reply.

'Are you hungry?'

Her brown hair may have given a little shake.

'I'll put some lunch on the table and then you can help yourself when you feel like it.'

I ate some sandwiches myself and had a bowl of buttermilk. As I ate I noticed the rain was easing off. The sky was clearing and there were patches of blue between the grey clouds. Further out on the lake the sun was actually shining. Fjuk was bathed in light. Then the rain suddenly stopped, like a bathroom shower being turned off.

'I'm going outside for a bit,' I called.

Standing on the step and wondering how to make a wheelchair ramp, I had a brilliant idea. I could use an ordinary door! One of the flat internal ones.

I went over to the outhouse to see whether there were any spare doors, but there weren't. My eyes lit instead on the grey one to the store cupboard where the chicken feed was kept. That would be perfect.

I lifted it off its hinges and carried it across the garden on my head. I laid it down to try it, like a bridge from the threshold and over the low step on to the lawn. All that was needed were a couple of nails at the upper end to hold it in place.

I took the longest nails I could find and hammered them in at an angle through the door and into the house wall.

Stepping back into the garden to inspect the ramp, I was dead chuffed with myself: it looked really good. It wasn't too steep for Mary-Lou to be able to wheel herself in and out whenever she wanted.

'Come and have a test-drive, Mary-Lou!' I shouted.

To my surprise I heard the wheelchair starting to move inside the house.

'Adam's Agency, at your service,' I said as Mary-Lou appeared in the porch.

Her face was expressionless as she rolled forward and paused on the threshold. Then she went slowly ahead over the grey door.

'Yeah, that's fine,' she said, continuing into the garden.

She pushed herself over to the chicken coop and I remembered I had to let out Siv and Ruth, so I followed her.

The chickens came flouncing out as fast as their legs would carry them, ruffling their feathers and sending clouds of dust into the air.

My success with the ramp certainly cheered me up. I sauntered around inside the house with Britt's ruler in my hand and a short stump of red pencil behind my ear, whistling to myself, periodically glancing out of the open door.

There was a lovely damp smell in the garden, the sun was filtering through the glistening leaves, the sky was completely cloudless. Mary-Lou was sitting by the chicken run in her chair. I couldn't make out whether she was asleep, but she certainly appeared to be. Every time I looked at her she was in exactly the same position, her head a little on one side.

Maybe she was thinking. Quite likely, because she seemed to do a lot of it. She worried about things all the time nowadays, going over everything repeatedly in her mind. It made me wonder whether it could be good for her. It might even be too much for her. If you only talk to yourself, inside your own head, you don't get any answers other than your own.

She seemed different somehow after the wheelchair dip. She was no longer so surly, nor so prickly. But she was very quiet and pensive, perhaps even more than ever.

Which was why I was so surprised by what happened that afternoon.

I'd moseyed up to the privy to see whether adapting it for the handicapped would be easily within the competence of Adam's Agency. I stood sucking my pencil and could see it was a major undertaking. The stony path up to it was far too big a task, and there wasn't much that could be done about the little wooden hut itself. There was no point in trying to put a ramp in if you couldn't get a wheelchair up there in the first place. And the hut was so small that a wheelchair wouldn't fit in anyway.

I started envisaging ways of constructing an aerial ropeway up to it from the cottage, with a basket to sit in and turned by a crank handle. But I would need a steel cable for that, or at least a really strong rope and some sort of pulley for it to run through. Which I hadn't got. But maybe could get hold of.

It was about then that I was woken from my musings by a peal of laughter from the garden below. It didn't register as that immediately, but rather just as a sound I recognised. A fragment of voice. A memory awakened. The question was: whose voice? For a split second I was three years younger again and sitting in the Bronze Age meadow. Mary-Lou was whirling around me and saying, '*You're going to be an artist, Adam.*' And then her laughter, like a clear babbling brook.

Equally abruptly the memory was overlaid by the laughter from the garden. It was Mary-Lou's laugh, of course! And then her voice.

'Adam, come and see! I've got something to show you.'

I went racing down to her. I couldn't understand what could have happened. She was sitting by the chicken coop in her wheelchair exactly as she'd been sitting all afternoon. She'd turned to face me and seemed excited, and I could see she had something to tell me, something that couldn't wait. For a moment I thought it really was the old Mary-Lou back again, direct from my memory into the present.

'What's up?'

'It's the hens.'

'What about them?'

'They're not moulting.'

'Aren't they?'

'No, they're fine. They're laying all right.'

'They are?'

'Yes. Just as they have been all summer.'

'How do you know?'

Mary-Lou pointed at the chicken coop.

'Not in the car,' she said. 'Underneath it.'

I got down on my knees and looked where she was indicating, under the Volvo. And there was a large basin-shaped hollow in the brown earth. And the hollow was full of eggs.

'There must be dozens of them!' I burst out in astonishment.

Mary-Lou didn't say a word. She was laughing too much.

There was something magical about those eggs. There weren't several dozen. But there were twenty-two in total. They almost filled the wooden rack in the larder. What was magical was the effect they had on Mary-Lou. It was the eggs that brightened her up, it was the eggs that made her laugh. Though I soon realised it wasn't only that – it was the wheelchair dip too. That was what jolted her out of her apathy, made her reassess her attitude. The chickens were just the final touch. They were the catalyst.

Though really I didn't think it was the dip either. Not that alone. Because the laughter was in her when she arrived. It was locked in, right down in the depths of her soul. But it wanted to get out. Maybe that was why she came.

I stood in the kitchen whisking four eggs with eight tablespoons of water in a plastic bowl. Added salt and pepper and a few drops of ketchup. Poured half the mixture into a hot frying pan. The oil sizzled.

I melted two tablespoons of butter in another pan, sprinkled in a handful of flour and pretended not to notice that it was snowing flour all over the stove. A little milk, brought it back to a simmer, stirred in more milk as it thickened. Then I emptied a tin of asparagus in.

When the first omelette was golden brown I slid it out on to a plate. It landed neatly and I covered it with a good helping of the asparagus concoction I'd made and folded the omelette in half over it. I put the plate in front of Mary-Lou. She took a sniff.

'Wow, what a marvellous smell. You're a terrific cook, Adam.'

'I like food. Cooking can be fun.'

As we ate I reminded her we'd soon be able to go mushrooming. With the amount of rain we'd had, there ought to be lots.

'Omelette with chanterelle mushrooms is fantastic,' I said wistfully.

Mary-Lou agreed. She wiped her plate with a piece of bread and crammed it in her mouth avidly.

'Or parasol mushrooms,' I went on. 'There are usually some over at the Bronze Age.'

But at that she burst out laughing again. I could hear a deep rumble somewhere inside her and the laughter working its way up and exploding in her mouth like a joyous volcanic eruption.

'What's the matter?'

But she couldn't stop laughing. She buried her face in her hands, her whole body quivering, tears streaming down her cheeks, until, finally managing to pull herself together and wiping her eyes, she said, 'I was thinking about you pushing me out into the water. It was a good thing you did that, Adam.'

'Honestly?'

She nodded.

'I was utterly insufferable. But it wasn't aimed at you. I can't really explain it. I think it was a mask I had to wear. I needed to put up some defence mechanism to dare to come here at all. I didn't mean to scare you. I was just so angry.'

'I wasn't scared.'

As I wrote in my diary I could sense Mary-Lou reading over my shoulder: *15°, torrential rain, wind light north-easterly. 22 eggs!*

'Haven't you got a rain gauge?' she asked.

'To think that hens can be so crafty,' I said.

I was woken by noises from the kitchen and immediately tensed up, until I remembered Mary-Lou was here. It was light outside so I assumed it was morning but I had no idea what the time was. I stayed in my warm bed, drowsing, trying to imagine what she might be doing that would sound like that.

The larder door had creaked several times and now I thought the noise was mostly coming from the table. She was whisking something. Eggs? Presumably. Eventually I heard the wheelchair move across the kitchen floor, the cupboard door open and close. My door was ajar and I caught a glimpse of her with a bag of sugar in her hands. Then the whisk started up again. She must be baking, I thought. She must be baking a cake. But before I could get excited about it I slipped groggily back into the land of dreams.

It was the telephone that woke me next. Several insistent rings echoing through the cottage. I sat up in bed, with a feeling of having been in a really deep sleep, the way you can be when you finally relax after feeling apprehensive. Just as I was about to drag myself out of bed I remembered that we didn't have a telephone in the house. Only my dad's mobile – and he had that with him.

I lay where I was, trying to bring myself round. It was still ringing, but now I could hear that it was actually Mary-Lou.

'Hallo, yes?' I shouted, in an attempt to get it to stop.

'Is that Adam's Taxis?'

I grinned to myself. Got the joke.

'Yes, it is,' I croaked.

'Could I have a taxi to the bee house?'

'To the bee house: that'll be . . . '

I was very near to drifting off again, but the sudden realisation dawned on me that Mary-Lou needed to go to the toilet. I climbed out of bed, pulled on my jeans, stumbled out to the kitchen. She was sitting there laughing at me. The table was full of gadgets, bowls, packs of margarine and bags of sugar and eggshells. There was a strong aroma of baking.

'How you sleep! It's half past ten!'

'Really?'

She nodded.

'I've baked a peach cake,' she said.

'What's that?'

'You can try it. Soon.'

She rolled out into the porch, opened the door and continued cautiously down the ramp. I followed her out and brought the wheelbarrow over from where it was leaning against the wall. She raised herself and I helped her into it. I noticed I was finding it easier to manoeuvre her now. I must have got more used to it. But I also thought she must be doing more for herself than she had at the beginning.

'Hold tight,' I said, setting off up the stony path.

We ate all the peach cake for breakfast. It was too good to leave, and there was only the tiniest triangle remaining that Mary-Lou said Ruth and Siv should have.

'You'll have to show me how to make it sometime,' I said, really impressed by her recipe. She'd made the same mixture as for an apple cake, but if you hadn't got any apples you substituted whatever you happened to have in the kitchen: bananas, melon, cucumber maybe, or even chocolates. In this case it had been a tin of peaches from my father's store.

While I was washing up after her morning bake, she disappeared down to the hens. I had put her cup outside on the bench in front of the house, because I'd noticed that she always liked a few more sips of coffee after I'd finished drinking.

'They loved it,' she shouted through the open door.

'Cool!'

I cleaned the table and swept the floor, since there was a lot of sugar crunching underfoot. Mary-Lou called through the window this time, 'Adam . . .'

'Yes?'

'Shall we go out somewhere?'

'Where to?'

'I don't know. To the Bronze Age, perhaps, if we can manage to get there.'

Even as we were making our way through the woods I could feel there would be something special about this day. The sun streamed through the tall firs on to the moss and the few ground plants. A swarm of gnats was dancing against the light like a living cloud.

'You feel as small as an ant,' said Mary-Lou, squinting up at the treetops that seemed to reach halfway to the sky.

One little worker ant pushing another little worker ant in a wheelchair, I thought. There were a lot of protruding roots that the two little ants had to negotiate. They lay across the path like stout arms. I'd never noticed them before. I'd never dreamt that I would one day be pushing a wheelchair up this path.

'You okay?' I asked when we hit a particularly awkward patch and my sketchpad had dropped to the ground.

'Yeah, sure. This is fantastic, Adam. I love these woods.'

'I know, it's brilliant,' I said, scooping up the pad and handing it to Mary-Lou. And with a nod towards the ancient trees, 'It's like walking through a John Bauer picture.'

John Bauer was my idol when I was younger. My dad had a whole drawer full of old Christmas magazines illustrated by him. I tried to draw like him for several years. I trained myself to imitate the style of his pictures of dark forests peopled by big kindly trolls and beautiful dainty princesses. I put tracing paper over the pages and copied them. Then I tried without tracing paper. Eventually I came to feel I was part of his world, in his forests. I thought I understood his methods. It was his pictures that made me dream of learning to draw properly, of becoming an artist like him.

I felt the urge to tell Mary-Lou about it.

'He really could make you feel how insignificant we are compared with nature.'

'Who?'

'John Bauer. Every tree stump in his forests is alive. He opens up new dimensions, creates new worlds.'

It took a lot longer than I expected to get to the meadow. It was hard work navigating through the woods. I felt like the captain of a ship. I sometimes tacked between the trees off the path to avoid a root or a boulder. Sometimes I had to tilt the front upwards, as if mounting a kerb. It reminded me of a computer game. You mustn't trip over or you'll be shot.

When the woods opened out before us and we saw the broad meadow stretched out in the sun, it felt a bit unreal at first. It was as if we'd travelled in a time machine. Mary-Lou was twelve when she was last here. She had flown like the summer breeze among the flowers and the burial mounds. She was so lively, so alive. I could still remember her as she was then: her voice, her quick movements, her laughter. All that was still there in me. Was still there in the meadow. And now I was back here with her in a wheelchair. As an invalid. As one of the living dead. No, not that. Not any more. But as a handicapped person. Like a butterfly without wings.

'It's delightful,' she exclaimed. 'It's just as I remember it.'

It was turning into a really strange day. Not because anything special happened. Or maybe precisely because of that. Because nothing much happened. And yet everything happened, again. I thought so, anyhow.

To me the meadow seemed like a picture frozen in time: from the day when Mary-Lou threw herself out of her cherry tree. Nothing had been touched since then. Nothing had moved, nothing had been added or taken away. Everything was the same. The same as then. That was how it felt to me. I set my feet on the grass with reverence.

Mary-Lou didn't seem to experience it so solemnly at all. For her it was a fond reunion. She said, 'Oh, how lovely,' when we parked next to a flowering dog-rose bush. I broke off a rose.

'To the prettiest girl in the meadow,' I said as I gave it to her.

She laughed as she took it, closed her eyes and smelt it.

'Do you remember I gave you a drawing of one of these?'

'No,' she said in surprise, 'I don't remember it at all.'

'I'd drawn a bud that was half out. Then I wrote *To Mary-Lou* on it. And gave it to you.'

'What a shame I haven't still got it.'

'I'll do you another one. I'm much better at it now.'

'Do you still draw as many flowers?'

'Only when I'm here. There's something remarkable about flowers, they're living organisms, they're individuals. Almost like people. But you don't notice it until you look at them closely. You have to learn to see before you can learn to draw.'

I paused, surveying the meadow.

'Flowers are the earth's eyes,' I went on.

'How do you mean?'

'Just look around you, Mary-Lou. Can't you see them watching us? They've been doing it ever since they heard us on the path. Look at the harebells over there in the shade and the daisies right by you. They can see us.'

Mary-Lou said nothing. She must have been thinking over what I'd said: that flowers are the earth's eyes. Maybe she was thinking it was a beautiful expression. Romantic. Like an ancient dream that people had long ago. A dream of a better world, perhaps.

'Do you think they recognise us?' she asked.

'Of course. Flowers can be very old. There are some that are hundreds of years old and come out in the same place every year. It's exactly the same plants growing here now as when we were here last. Of course they recognise us.'

'Hi,' said Mary-Lou, looking down at some lady's bedstraw right by us. 'Sorry about this chair.'

'I'm not joking, Mary-Lou. I really think it's like that. There's much more to life than we're aware of. Flowers are part of it. They have senses, just like us. They can see and feel. Every mindless act we commit against living things makes the flowers grieve.'

I fell silent and Mary-Lou said no more either. I took out my sketchpad and started drawing. I believed what I'd said to Mary-Lou. It felt like having living models in front of me. No two flowers were alike.

Mary-Lou wheeled herself in great loops around the meadow. She kept to the driest parts where the ground was firm and the grass short. She circled one of the burial cairns and came heading back towards me.

'Did you find anything?' I called.

She looked up.

'Like what?'

'Something that no one has ever found before.'

'What did you mean about finding something?' Mary-Lou asked when we were lying on the steep hillside.

'That's what you always used to say when we were here. You used to run about scrabbling in those old stone cairns declaring your intentions of making a find. You were going to discover something that no one had ever found before. And you said you wanted to be an archaeologist. I've often thought of that. You ought to come back here and excavate them properly.'

'Did I really?' she said, quite astounded. 'Archae-ologist! I don't remember it. I only remember playing with the stones. And you sitting somewhere nearby drawing flowers. And us lying here and looking out across the lake, because you were always nervous about looking down. Are you still?'

'Sure. You don't grow out of vertigo, more's the pity. It's actually a bit worse. I'm ashamed of that and of the fact that I can't swim. Though that's Britt Börjesson's fault. Like lots of things.'

Mary-Lou sat in silence watching a sea-going yacht with a blue mainsail gliding over the water far below us. There was bright white foam at the bows.

'Life is weird,' she said. 'The last time we were together I was twelve and the way I used to sail a dinghy the water would be dripping off the sail for hours after-wards. That's what I remember dreaming of, sailing. Sailing round the world.'

I said nothing. Couldn't think of anything suitable. Mary-Lou carried on talking.

'And now I'm fifteen and in a wheelchair. There won't be any round-the-world sailing. And not much else either. I remember dreaming about the Eiffel Tower. I think my mum and dad must have talked about going to Paris on holiday. I probably won't get there either. At least not up the Tower. I haven't got any extra energy for things like that. No energy for anything. It's as if part of me has withered away.'

She fell silent. I had to say something.

'But you're still the same person. Though three years

older, of course. You're a normal fifteen-year-old girl. This isn't important,' I said, kicking at the wheelchair.

'No, not for somebody who doesn't need one. But you're right in a sense. I'm getting used to it. I'm not thinking all the time that I'm in a wheelchair. I often think about quite normal things, like boys. I even think I might be able to sail again. The problem is that I can't be bothered any more. I know there's a lift in the Eiffel Tower because my schoolfriend Mona is always rabbiting on about it. So I know. Nearly everything is adapted for the handicapped now. You can go round the whole damned world in a wheelchair. But that's not the point. That's not what's so hard. Getting in and out of buses and shops and toilets. They're problems you can overcome. It's me that's the problem. It's me that doesn't work. My brain isn't adapted to handicap. Sometimes I get so depressed that I can't bear myself. It goes off after a while, luckily. And I'm not usually as pathetic as I was when I arrived.'

She paused. Took a deep breath before declaring, 'Anyway, I'm not fifteen yet. My birthday's next week.'

'Then we'll have a party,' I said.

'Okay, if you like,' said Mary-Lou.

I pushed myself laboriously through the garden, trying to stick to the path, but it was so overgrown with grass that it was actually bumpier than the lawn. I continued out on to the jetty and it was much easier there. This is how it should be, I thought. This is how it should be everywhere. I rested for a while. My arms were nearly

84

giving out. Then I changed my grip and manoeuvred myself over towards the outhouse. Here and there the wheels dipped into some invisible hollow in the unmown grass, and once I almost toppled forward right out of the wheelchair. I had never realised there were so many uneven patches in our lawn. I was wet with sweat.

I hunted for my father's motor mower, which was buried under a load of plastic bags full of empty wine bottles waiting for recycling. The mower was a real monster, at least twenty years old and meant for professional use in parks. It was incredibly powerful and would go through anything: nettles, bushes, washing that had blown off the line, bags of barbecue charcoal, slippers or anything else that had got lost in the grass. It was perfect for a lawn that was only cut a few times a year. My dad loved it. He had discovered it in a store-room at the newspaper office. It had been thrown out for scrap and he got it for nothing.

Searching for the petrol can, I came across the rain gauge on a shelf. I tucked it in my back pocket.

When I'd filled the mower I had an idea that I couldn't resist putting to the test. If I could couple the wheelchair behind the lawnmower, it ought to be possible to drive along behind and steer it. Like the ride-on mowers that nearly everyone had nowadays. Only more audacious. The world's first lawnmower for the handicapped! This was a job for Adam's Agency.

I experimented with several different designs before I found one I felt was reliable. Just tying the two together with a rope or chain, my first abortive attempt, was a dismal failure. The wheelchair had to be attached to the mower much more rigidly.

I eventually found four wide aluminium struts that must have belonged to some old bookshelving. I fixed them on with hose clips and screwed them so tight that I nearly ripped the threads off. I put two of the struts as low as they would go, because I reckoned this was where most of the stress would be.

I tried pushing the mower across the concrete and the wheelchair followed along obediently behind.

I turned on the petrol tap, opened the rusty throttle lever to maximum and pulled the start cord. The engine coughed. I pulled again, with the same result. My dad used to say it always started on the third attempt. He was sure there must be a gremlin in the machine. I could see him standing there, with a smile of satisfaction on his face, the engine roaring. Okay, Dad, here goes, I thought, and pulled the cord. The engine clattered into life with a hell of a din, spitting out a cloud of soot. I eased off the throttle and let the motor idle for a while. Then I sat myself in the wheelchair, leant forward and increased the throttle to 'max', shifted the clutch to 'go' and trundled out across the lawn.

The mower followed the steering in a dead straight line, cutting all the grass in its path. I was poised on tenterhooks at first, but when I felt it was going to work I sat back in the seat. Mary-Lou was at the kitchen window with a book in her hand pointing at me and doubled up with laughter. I waved to her. Then I wondered whether she was managing to walk a little by herself, because she had been lying on her bed reading when I came out.

I must have been lost in a world of my own, because all of a sudden the chair heeled over and I was flung out on to the grass, while the mower continued on its merry way.

As I went racing after it I could hear tapping on the window. Mary-Lou was convulsed with mirth.

Unhitching the wheelchair took almost as long as making the contraption. When I'd done I looked up at the window. I gestured at the wheelchair and then at Mary-Lou, but she shook her head so I parked it in among the sour-cherry bushes.

I continued with the mowing. The heavy machine had no problem coping with the uneven grass. I just walked behind it and kept a watch in front so that I wouldn't run into anything. One summer my dad drove it right through Britt's sacred herb garden. After that he set up a pole with a white T-shirt on, in the middle of the garden. But it was gone now. As far as I knew, Britt hadn't been growing anything for the last few years. As far as I knew, she wasn't here all that often any more either.

Mowing the slope up towards the privy I saw a swarm of bees emerge from the border of stones where the lawn ended and nature took over. So, it's here you live, I thought to myself. When I turned for a final cut along the edge of the lawn even more bees appeared. They seemed disturbed but not angry. Not like wasps, anyway. When several of them headed directly for the mower I made one final swing and came back down the garden.

After I turned off the mower outside the cottage it was as if someone switched on the summer again. A blissful silence descended on the garden. I could hear the faint sound of music from inside the house, the gulls squabbling by the jetty and the ceaseless lapping of the waves on the shore.

The lawn was far from perfect. Where it was wet, the mower had just torn at it. In future I would use the little hand-mower Britt had bought. It worked well when the grass was short.

'It'll be a lot better next time,' I called out to Mary-Lou.

She was sitting at the window and closed her book as I came in.

'What a shame your invention was no good,' she said with a smile.

'Or fortunate,' I replied. 'It was absolutely deafening.'

I was about to say how hungry I was when I felt something in my back pocket.

'Oh, I found this, by the way.'

Mary-Lou was overjoyed, as if it was an early birthday present rather than just a dirty old rain gauge.

We were drinking buttermilk and eating tomato and cucumber sandwiches on the jetty. It was the end of the bread and I was thinking I mustn't forget to cycle to the supermarket before it closed. We were feeding the perch and laughing as they darted out of the black recesses under the boulders to gobble up our crumbs. It was hot in the sun and when I'd taken our plates and things back in we just sat relaxing there on the jetty. I'd changed into my swimming trunks and could see my body had begun to get a bit of colour. I wondered about fetching something to read, but it was too much trouble. The boat gurgled at its mooring as the swell from a passing motorboat reached us. I opened my eyes and scanned the lake. Fjuk was hovering like the Flying Dutchman; the island looked as if it was several metres above the surface.

'When I was little I thought Fjuk was bewitched. It seemed to be always shifting from one place to another.'

Mary-Lou laughed at me.

'There aren't any such things as bewitched islands, Adam. But if there were, I'm sure Fjuk would be one. I sailed there once. It's a weird place. It felt as if time stood still out there. Like it can feel up at the Bronze Age. A man once used to live in a wooden cabin all alone on the island. The hermit of Fjuk.'

'Like me.'

'You're not alone.'

'I was.'

'The hermit lived out there all his life. Not just one summer.'

'What was his name, this hermit? What was he called?'

'I don't know. I've never heard anyone say anything except "the hermit". I think it sounds rather nice.'

Mary-Lou stretched herself like a cat that's been woken up and can't decide whether to go back to sleep or not.

'The water's very tempting,' she remarked indolently.

'Come on, then. I'll help you.'

'I know,' she said with a grimace.

'I ought to teach myself to swim,' I said. 'I'd thought I might try to learn this summer.'

'I can help you,' said Mary-Lou.

'How?'

'Give you instructions. It's hard to learn to swim on your own.'

'I know what to do,' I said.

'Show me then!'

I sat up. Made some swimming movements with my arms. But she stopped me.

'In the water, stupid. And you'll have to make your arm strokes bigger. You're only going halfway. Look, like this!'

She did several strokes in the air. Sweeping her arms in a wide arc round the wheelchair.

'You're just pushing your arms out in front of you,' she said. 'That won't work. You'll sink like a stone.'

'How's this, then?' I said, trying to imitate her circular arm movements.

'That's a lot better. In you go.'

I hopped off the jetty and stood in the water. It came up above my trunks. It was colder than I'd expected and I hesitated for a minute before plunging in. I did a few hurried arm strokes before standing up again.

'Did you see that?'

Mary-Lou roared with laughter.

'Haven't you got any water-wings?'

'Afraid not.'

'Then you'd better dream up something else.'

'A board?'

'That might do.'

I left the water and went over to the outhouse. I knew there would be some wooden planks there but also some sheets of stiff white polystyrene from when Britt insulated the porch. I found a piece nearly twenty centimetres wide and more than a metre long.

When I came back with the polystyrene I went straight into the water with it. I positioned myself on it carefully, so that it was under my stomach, below the ribs. I could feel it supporting my weight and began to do some rapid strokes with my arms.

'Slower, Adam!' Mary-Lou shouted.

I slowed down and did a few more strokes, but soon had to stand up because my head was starting to go under.

'Good! Go on!'

I felt ridiculous playing at swimming lessons. I was fifteen after all. But it was even more wimpish not being able to swim. I'd suffered enough for that already, so I supposed I could put up with a bit more. I lay on the board again and practised some more strokes. It didn't feel as if I was moving forward but as if the board and I were turning a slow circle in the water. I managed to keep going longer this time before I felt my head sinking.

'That's better, Adam,' Mary-Lou called as I stood up. 'The last few strokes were really ace. I think you should just lie on it now and splash about or do whatever you want. So you get used to it and feel that you're floating. That'll get rid of your fear.'

'It's not fear.'

I waded across to the jetty, pushing the board ahead of me. Flicked it up beside her.

'Do you think I'll be able to learn, then?'

'If you practise every day you'll soon be swimming like a fish.'

Her words reminded me of something I'd completely forgotten.

'The net!' I yelled, so loud that it made her jump. 'I'd forgotten the net! It's been in the water I don't know how long. Hell, what if it's full of dead fish?'

'Where is it?'

'Just beyond the point, to the south.'

'The water's icy cold out there, the fish will stay alive for ages.'

'You think so?'

I had trouble concentrating on anything else after that. I wanted to row out immediately but Mary-Lou said there was no real hurry now they'd been there so long anyway. She wanted to go in the water. Though after thinking it over she seemed to lose her enthusiasm or something, because then she said it didn't matter.

'Do you want to come with me?'

She shook her head.

'No,' she said. 'But fish tonight would be fab. It's ages since I had char.'

I felt rather downcast as I rowed the heavy boat out to

the point. I was ashamed, felt guilty. I couldn't help thinking of Mary-Lou's carefree talk about char. So typical of her, never worrying about anything. That was how she had always been. Or rather, that was how she'd been in the old days. If there were any fish in the net they'd be way beyond their last gasp.

I must have a talent for magnifying things in my mind, because after a while my head was full, like a whole videotape. A nauseating picture of mutilated fish trapped in an old nylon net floating around in the water. The fish had staring unseeing white eyes. Some of them were gashed by the nylon threads scoring deep into their flesh, others were half rotted with their fins dropping off. Ghost nets, I believe they're called. I read in an article in the paper once that there are thousands of ownerless nets drifting about in the best fishing grounds, forgotten or ripped loose by storms. But this was my own ghost net, the guilty owner was Adam.

The first problem was to find it. It wasn't where I thought I'd laid it, if I could really think anything at all, since I hadn't noted any landmarks.

I rowed about aimlessly, standing up at intervals to inspect the glassy surface of the lake. I had almost decided to give up, assuming that someone else must have noticed the net had been there a long time and had taken it in. Perhaps there's an unwritten law on the subject. But just as I was going to head back to shore I thought I caught sight of something way out on the lake. I rowed over and was astonished to find it was actually my plastic buoy. I was certain it must have become detached and drifted here on its own, because I couldn't have laid the net so far offshore.

Yet when I pulled the red buoy out of the water I found the net still attached. With trembling hands I began hauling it in. A few experimental tugs: it felt quite heavy. Hell. What if the whole net was full of one great sludge of putrefying fish? Whitefish and char and pike and grayling and perch... The mere thought of it made me want to retch.

As the first threads of nylon came in over the gunwale I could see they were clean. No trace of dead or damaged fish. I took heart and went on slowly dragging it in, piling it up in the centre of the boat, because in my agitated state I'd forgotten to bring the spool.

The net continued emerging from the dark waters. The threads looked untouched, the drops of water on them glistening like pearls. Could it really be true? When my dad came ashore with empty nets, which happened pretty often, he'd always grumble that someone had been there first and emptied them. Which wouldn't have been beyond the bounds of possibility since he seldom went out on the lake till late afternoon.

But now? In a net that had been floating around for so long? I leant over the side and peered down hopefully into the water. Nothing, not a glimmer of a fish. So I went on hauling it in and as the pile grew so my humour improved. When the end of the net came into sight I was inwardly jubilant.

I rowed the heavy vessel back as if it was made of

light resin. When I got to the jetty I was still brimming over with joy. I stood up in the boat.

'Mary-Lou!' I cried. 'Mary-Lou, it was empty! Not a single fish! Fantastic luck!' I came ashore and dumped the net in the plastic bowl where I'd found it, vowing never to use it ever again.

Mary-Lou seemed neither surprised nor pleased. She'd guessed as much, she said.

'You can't just put out a net any old where and think you'll get masses of fish. The lake is too big for that. It's more than a hundred metres deep.'

'So do you know where it's best to fish?'

She nodded.

'I knew once, anyway. We can try and see if it's still the same.'

'I'm not so keen any more.'

'Well, you don't have to do it.'

'True.'

I stood at the stove heating up a tin of potatoes with dill and a tin of fish balls in cheese and paprika sauce. When I'd remembered the net, I'd forgotten I needed to go out and do some shopping. Typical of me. This was the best the house could offer. I spooned out some fishballs and arranged the potatoes beside them.

'One char, madam,' I said, serving Mary-Lou with a flourish.

She laughed. Then she gave me a long look while I let the water run cold from the tap. I felt it with my finger and filled a glass carafe.

'I'll buy some lemons in the morning,' I said. 'Then we can make lemonade. Provided I don't go and forget.'

She had stopped looking at me. She was chasing a potato round her plate, made a sudden attack and speared it with her fork. She chewed it suspiciously, with the slightest hint of a wrinkle above her nose. Swallowing it, she said, 'You're a weird sort of guy, Adam. Did you know that?'

The next morning I woke up early. The sun was shining and I crept out of bed silently, took off my underpants, hung them on the bedside lamp and tiptoed into the kitchen. Not a sound from Mary-Lou's room. I opened the outer door quietly, ran naked down to the beach and went straight in the water.

It was bitterly cold of course, but since I wasn't properly awake I didn't notice it until I was already in. And since the air was still cool and fresh the difference wasn't as great as it would be later in the day. It was when I stood up again in the waist-high water that I really felt it.

I wasn't in the habit of taking a morning dip. It wasn't really my style. In fact I usually needed to sit around for an hour before I could do anything at all. It must have been because I'd been thinking about Mary-Lou's swimming lessons and my polystyrene board that I'd decided to go down to the lake. I must also have had the idea of getting in some practice on the board. But I knew immediately that I'd picked the wrong time of day. I just took the board into the water and lay on it briefly before I started to freeze and hastily came out again.

I glanced up at the window of Mary-Lou's room but there was no sign of life. I stopped by the ramp and tried to clean my feet that were green with grass cuttings, but they were stuck on and almost impossible to get off. When I tried rubbing with my hands the grass just transferred itself to them instead.

In the larder there were only eggs or tins to choose from, so I took four eggs and scrambled them in a saucepan. I added salt and pepper and a sprinkling of Britt's dried basil that was hanging on the wall. I boiled the water. Put cream crackers on the table and a squashed tube of shrimp paste that I found lurking at the back of the fridge.

'Are you awake?' I called. 'Breakfast is ready.'

I heard movement. A few minutes passed and then the door opened and in she rolled. She had a long white T-shirt on and looked very sleepy. Her hair was all tangled up on the top of her head like spaghetti.

I grinned.

'The bee house?'

She nodded and made an effort to stand, like a sleep-walker. I put my arms round her and carried her out of the cottage and lowered her into the wheelbarrow.

'Do you know why wheelbarrows only have one wheel?'

She shook her head. Her hair dropped down and fell into place.

'Because they were invented by a Scot who was too miserly to pay for two.'

Mary-Lou looked at me doubtfully. 'Did they really come from Scotland?'

Then her eyes slowly cleared as my joke sank in.

'You're making it up, Adam, it's not true!'

I shrugged my shoulders and she began to giggle. A high-pitched, hysterical giggle.

I smiled at her, grabbed the wooden handles and set off gently up to the privy. She was still giggling, but I wasn't sure whether it was at my feeble joke or at something else.

'I've been in the lake already,' I said. 'I've been swimming.'

'You're mad,' she said.

I made a list of things we needed: *milk, buttermilk, bread, cheese, tomatoes, lemons, onions, bananas, potatoes*. What else? Tried to prompt myself by going from room to room.

Mary-Lou was reading about perspective drawing. She seemed deeply engrossed in the subject and was sipping absent-mindedly at her coffee.

'Can you think of anything else?' I asked, reading out what I'd written.

'Loo paper. It's nearly all gone. And shampoo.'

'Brilliant,' I said, writing them down. 'More?'

'Apples, green ones, preferably.'

'Popcorn,' I added, because I liked that a lot.

'A small packet of Marlboro,' said Mary-Lou, scrutinising me again. She kept her eyes fixed on me. As if trying to assess my reaction.

I kept shtum. Just wrote: *Marlboro*.

'I think we get on pretty well together,' she said.

I nodded. 'I think so too, it's working out well. Much better than I'd expected.'

'It feels cosy being with you,' she went on. 'You're almost like a father. I wouldn't mind living like this. Staying here for ever.'

'Even in the winter, with heavy snow and ice a metre thick and power cuts . . . ?'

'Yes, even in the winter. We could make a fire in that old kitchen stove and light candles and sit reading in the evenings. I have a feeling there would be real peace and quiet here. In town I often try to imagine what other people do in the evenings. Not when they're at the cinema or McDonald's but when they're at home. What their Monday evenings are like. How they live their everyday lives. Do you know what I mean?'

I nodded because I thought I did. My weekday evenings at home were pure chaos.

'Where we live you can see right into the building opposite,' Mary-Lou continued. 'There's a whole wall of windows facing ours. I like sitting there in the evenings and looking into all the rooms that are lit and checking on what people are up to. It's probably not very polite, but I do it anyway. I've learnt their routines, so I know precisely what they should be doing. When they come home, when they eat, when they go to the loo, when they turn the lights out. It's a bit scary. That we repeat ourselves so much. You don't think about it yourself. You're not aware of your own life. But I can see the pattern so clearly when I sit there watching. You understand what I'm getting at?'

'Can you really see when they go to the loo?' I asked sceptically.

'I see them leave the room. I know that's what they must be doing.'

'My evenings aren't like that at all,' I interpolated. 'At least I don't think they are.'

But Mary-Lou wasn't interested in what my evenings were like.

'One couple are always sitting in front of the TV drinking coffee, there's one guy who makes pasta just dressed in his underpants, a girl who studies all evening curled up in a big armchair. An old lady does the ironing while she chats on the phone, an old man wanders around all day with no shirt on and keeps his window open till he turns off the light at half past nine every night. It's like a world in miniature. Have you ever spied on people?'

'I've never even thought of it. I wouldn't have time. In town I'm always dashing from one thing to another. Since my dad is as often as not away or working late I have to do everything. I do the shopping, cleaning, make the meals, do my homework, draw, train the hockey team. There isn't enough time for everything. I'm doing all the stuff that you're sitting and watching. Oh, yes, one thing I do fairly regularly when I come home is take the stairs instead of the lift just so I can go past the Larsens' on the third floor. There's always a smell of food. You know, I made it part of my routine for a while, I always made a meal the same as the smell from their flat. If the Larsens were cooking pork chops or grilled herring I would go straight out to the supermarket and buy two pork chops or a pack of herring.'

'What a cool idea!'

'Yeah, though you couldn't always be sure of what the smell was. I rang their bell and asked once. I told them exactly why, that it always smelt so good. The lady was really chuffed and started talking about this and that and said they were about to go out to a restaurant for her sister's sixtieth birthday.'

'So what was it then?'

'They were defrosting the freezer and cooking an old hare that they'd found right at the bottom. They were going to give it to her sister's dog.'

Mary-Lou chuckled, then turned serious again.

'I think that's what life's about, Adam. Finding your daily routine. At first you think everything should be as intense as possible. Discos, travel, beauty contests, parties, beaches. That's what I thought. That's what I dreamt about. About all the places I wanted to see. But then you come to realise that it's the opposite. Life consists of ninety per cent daily routines and ten per cent fun. Or something like that. Or am I wrong, Adam? Is it because I'm stuck in this damned chair that I think like that? To try and console myself?'

'I don't know,' I said in all honesty. 'It sounds sensible what you say about finding satisfaction in everyday life. It sounds grown-up. It's the sort of thing my mother would say.'

'Are you in contact with her?'

'We phone one another quite often. In the winter, at any rate. She lives up in the north, in Ljusdal. Did you know that?'

Mary-Lou shook her head.

'Is she a journalist too?'

'She's news editor on the local paper up there.'

Mary-Lou made no comment.

'Right, I'm off to the shop now,' I said. 'Can you let out Siv and Ruth and give them some food?'

'Sure.'

Before folding the piece of paper I added in tiny print: *Present*.

As I cycled past the long row of letter boxes by the bus stop I noticed the wind was getting up. The flaps were moving in the breeze. I thought it looked as if they were talking to one another. There was a white letter box at the far end whose jaw was going non-stop.

I opened the mouth of our box and found a letter. It was for Mary-Lou and when I turned it over I saw that it was from her mother, Irja. I stuffed it in my back pocket.

I went over in my mind what Mary-Lou had said about establishing your daily routine. It seemed rather alarming to me. I'd thought of giving a different answer when she asked me my opinion. But I knew I didn't dare. It sounds so sad, Mary-Lou, was what I'd wanted to say. You used to climb the highest trees, you used to go out sailing on the windiest days, you used to dream of climbing the Eiffel Tower and travelling round the world. What do you dream of now? Sitting contentedly in front of the TV on a bleak November evening?

It started raining when I was halfway there, of course. I was only wearing jeans and my blue sweater and was drenched by the time I got to the supermarket.

I stayed in the shop for ages. I browsed slowly along the shelves. Found more things to buy. Crispbread, stewed raspberries and whipped cream. But couldn't see any suitable present. What would Mary-Lou like? What did she need? I had no idea. I couldn't think of anything. When I finally made for the exit to pay the rain was worse.

'My God, what weather,' said Linda at the checkout. She gave me a smile, acknowledging my wet clothes. She had long curly hair and round-rimmed glasses and a green and white overall with her name embroidered on the left breast.

'Yeah,' I replied, peering out through the large rain-streaked windows.

I stayed for quite a while. Talked to Linda. Until it looked as if the worst was over. Then I left.

''Bye,' said Linda.

I was frozen cycling back. The rain might have stopped but the wind blew straight through my sodden clothes.

Opening the garden gate, I was aware that something was different. I couldn't work out what it was at first, because I was deep in thought about why John Bauer chose to make humans so small in his pictures.

But I soon sussed it. Siv and Ruth were strutting around on the lawn! Pausing every now and again, scratching with their feet, pecking with their beaks and hooking something up. Then on they strolled, chattering away about worms and seeds. They looked like two old ladies in grey headscarves.

At first I assumed Mary-Lou must have forgotten to shut the chicken run. Till it occurred to me that she hadn't forgotten at all. She'd let them out deliberately, of course!

They seemed to be looking at me accusingly as I passed. They clucked a little, as if telling me I could have done this ages ago.

'We'll talk about that later,' I said.

The cottage was empty. Mary-Lou's notepad was on the pine table by the window, but of her there was no sign. I stood for a few seconds at the table. Ran my finger over the brown cover of the notepad. Listened for Mary-Lou. Then I took off my wet clothes and went out and laid them on the bench. I got out my cut-off jeans and a T-shirt from the chest-of-drawers in my room.

I returned to the kitchen and unpacked what I'd bought. Felt a stab of annoyance when I remembered I hadn't got a present for Mary-Lou. I'd have liked to give her a book. A really good book. Poetry even. But they didn't have such things in the supermarket.

I was starving and made myself a cheese sandwich. Suddenly remembered I'd forgotten to buy any margarine. It was almost gone.

I picked up my sandwich and went out to find her. She was sitting behind the house, by the overgrown sour-cherry thicket. It was funny I hadn't seen her as I came in.

'Where have you been?' I asked.

'I've been for a pee.'

'Here on the lawn?'

'Over there,' she said, indicating the edge of the woods. 'Do you want me to show you the exact spot?'

'Did you manage on your own?' I asked in some surprise.

'It took one helluva time, Adam, but yes, I managed!'

I could hear from her voice that something was amiss. She sounded the way she had when she first arrived. Bitter and aggressive.

'What is it, Mary-Lou? Is everything all right?'

She was staring at me again, but not with that fond enquiring look. Not with eyes that liked me. This was just a glare.

'What do you want me to say? Don't you think I can cope for a few hours without something going wrong? Don't you, Adam? Do you think you're the one that makes everything work? Do you? Do you think it's your bloody wheelchair ramps that help me stay here? Do you? Answer me, Adam!'

I could feel myself beginning to lose my temper. I wanted to try and change the subject.

'Why did you let the hens out?'

Mary-Lou just stared at me. I realised too late that this would only make her worse.

'What do you mean? Shouldn't I have? Do you want those poor bloody hens imprisoned their whole lives? In a fucking car? You're off your head!'

'They're not imprisoned. That's their life. They feel

105

secure there. It's for their own good, as you well know. There are foxes around here, have you forgotten?'

'Foxes!' she snarled. 'Do you mean the hens have to live in that prison just because you're afraid of a fox?'

'Okay,' I said. 'They can go free as far as I'm concerned. But you'll have to take responsibility for them. You'll have to shut them in at night.'

'It'll be a pleasure!' Mary-Lou screamed.

With that she shoved herself off down the garden with hefty thrusts of her arms to where Siv and Ruth were ambling about. The wheelchair was coming straight at them and they had to hop out of the way, cackling in fright.

We were keeping a safe distance from one another. The weather was beginning to improve and when the sun came out in the afternoon I went down and lay on the jetty. I breathed in the scent of tar and cold clear lake water, and I think I must have dozed off to the sound of the swell against the boulders of the jetty. When I opened my eyes again I was quite warm. I decided to take a dip, tossed in my polystyrene swimming board and plunged in after it. I spent some time just trying to float with the board under me. It was difficult, but I found it was easier if I ventured some arm strokes, which seemed to give me more balance.

When I glanced up I saw Mary-Lou sitting on the jetty. I wondered how long she'd been there. She was looking down at me and was obviously in a better mood. Her eyes were softer, remorseful even.

'Adam...'

'Yeah?'

'Come up here.'

I waded through the water to the jetty, found a foothold and climbed up over the boulders.

'What?'

'Sorry, Adam. Sorry I was such an idiot.'

'Oh, that's okay.'

'I can't help myself. That's how I get sometimes. Full of uncontrollable rage over nothing.'

'I can understand. It's no big deal. You can get angry if you like.'

'You're so nice, Adam.'

I leant forward over the wheelchair and brought my face close to hers. I don't know why I did it. But it felt natural. My body seemed to act of its own accord. For a moment I was sure I was going to kiss her and I could see in her eyes that she thought so too. My mouth was so near to touching hers that I could feel her breath on my lips. But then something happened, I don't know what, and I brushed my hand over her cheek instead.

'You're nice too,' I said.

17°. Fresh breeze all day. Some rain (7mm). Two eggs. Hens liberated! It was Mary-Lou writing in the diary. I was leafing through it while drinking my morning tea. I felt stiff and thoroughly chilled and was having trouble waking up properly. I sneezed a couple of times and went to find a thicker sweater in my father's wardrobe, not sure whether I'd caught a cold or whether it was my

107

old dust allergy coming back. I went out and felt my blue sweater that was lying with my jeans on the bench outside the house. It was damp from the night air so I left it there. It would soon dry when the sun came round on to it.

Mary-Lou was still asleep. I assumed. I felt no desire to go in the water, even though the weather looked promising. The sun was halfway along the jetty. The lake was choppy, the water glinting and gleaming. Not real waves, not moving in any particular direction. Just wavelets playing around, before the wind got up and it was time for the day's journey.

Then I heard sounds of activity from Mary-Lou's room. I went to the stove and put on some more water and waited for her to emerge. To run my hand through her tangled hair. That's how our mornings began. We had no set routines, no rules or times, we let our bodies decide the rhythm. And yet: they always began like this.

Her crumpled morning face arrived at the door and I got up again to carry her out to Adam's bucking bronco, as she had christened it. I carried her in my arms, like a child, with one hand under her knees and the other behind her back. Very different from the beginning when I heaved her about like a statue.

It felt entirely natural for me to help Mary-Lou in all the situations where she needed physical support. I knew it was essential for her to go to the loo regularly, that that was one of her greatest daily anxieties. I think I was quite proud of myself. I've always been told I do everything so well. That I'm so mature and sensible for my age. It was true. I'd been standing on my own two feet for a long time. Ask my father! So I think I was the right person for all this.

And yet: this very morning I failed. I don't know why. Maybe because I was feeling stubborn, perhaps because we were still feeling shy of one another after the row of the day before. Our first fight!

Or perhaps it happened because I was trying to prove how well I was handling everything. Because I was getting blasé.

Just as I was carrying her down the ramp my right leg buckled under me. I couldn't tell whether it was my knee or cramp in my calf muscle that caused the problem. Perhaps I just put my foot down awkwardly. Anyway, my leg gave way and my whole body lurched to the right. If I'd been on my own it would have been easy to save myself. But with Mary-Lou in my arms the weight was too much for one leg. I kept my balance for a second or two but then down we went with a crash. I landed at some crazy angle with my head hanging off the ramp. Mary-Lou was lying higher up. Then I slid further down and ended up on the lawn. I felt my ear, and my fingers came away covered in blood.

Mary-Lou had got to her knees. She was holding on to the side of the house and laboriously trying to haul herself upright. It was taking for ever but she finally succeeded in standing.

'You okay?' I asked.

'Fine,' she said. 'What about you?'

'Nosebleed and split ear.'

'It's bleeding a lot.'

'So I see.'

As I wiped my hand on the grass I saw Mary-Lou leaning against the door frame, gripping it with both hands and extremely cautiously taking small shuffling steps into the doorway. I watched in amazement.

I raised myself to a sitting position. Blood was dripping on to my T-shirt. I had to get some kitchen paper. I tried to hold my T-shirt under my nose and tottered up the ramp.

'Can you manage?' I asked.

'No sweat.'

As I passed her I thought I saw her body trembling. I went into the kitchen and tore off several metres of kitchen roll. Turned on the tap and splashed water over my face. Folded the paper into a thick wad and held it up to my nose. Then I went back to Mary-Lou. The ramp was spattered with blood. My nose was still pouring and the paper was already crimson.

I pondered the next move. There was nothing I could do for Mary-Lou till my nosebleed had stopped.

'You ought to lie flat,' she said.

'Shall I get the wheelchair?'

She nodded.

When I came back I helped her into it.

'Go and lie down on the bed,' she said.

I did as instructed. Lay still with my nose in the air. Closed my eyes. Mary-Lou sat beside me, holding my hand.

'Do me a favour and turn off the stove,' I said.

We started again from the beginning. I lifted her into the wheelbarrow. Trudged up the path. Sat by the water's edge. Waited an eternity. As usual. Two gulls were squabbling over a dead fish they'd found on the beach. I wondered how it had died.

I made coffee, watching her spread two slices of bread with the margarine I'd saved for her. And all the time my brain was reviewing the sight it had registered earlier: Mary-Lou in the doorway, taking small steps. Maybe they weren't real steps, more like sliding her feet along. But there was one thing I would like to know. Something I'd been wanting to ask her for a long time. Something I didn't know about her handicap. And another thing related to it. It was hard to work out how best to broach it, how to find a natural way to talk about such a sensitive subject. I ruminated on the problem in silence.

'What's the matter, Adam?'

Thanks, Mary-Lou.

'I was thinking about when we fell over, and then right afterwards, when I was lying on the grass bleeding. It almost looked as if you actually walked a step or two . . .'

'What was going on there, do you mean?'

I could tell from her tone that she was waiting to pounce. Like a bird of prey with its eyes on a little mouse far below in the grass.

'I didn't think you could.'

'Could what?'

'Walk.'

111

'Do you call that walking?'

'Not exactly, but I'd never thought that someone in a wheelchair might be able to walk. Walk at all, I mean. I've never known anyone with a handicap before.'

'I've got feet, you know!'

'Yes, but...'

'And if I shuffle them along a few inches for once, you think that's a big thing, eh? Is that it?'

'No, that's not it at all. I just wondered how it works. If you can walk even a tiny bit, does that mean there's a chance you might be able to walk more at some time in the future?'

'No, Adam, it doesn't.'

'Can you know that for certain?'

'It's my spine I've broken, Adam.'

I thought I saw a barely discernible and slightly disparaging glance at the bright red wad of paper in my hand. At my nosebleed.

'I know, but you sometimes hear of people with really serious injuries making a recovery.'

'There's no such thing as miracles.'

'I'm not talking about miracles, Mary-Lou. I'm talking about people who've regained some movement in parts of their body after years of systematic exercise...'

Mary-Lou said nothing. So I completed my thought.

'Do you think you could? If you exercised like that?'

'How should I know? I can move my feet sometimes. When I relax. Or when I make a real effort. It varies. Sometimes they don't respond at all.'

'Have you tried doing regular exercise?'

'For three years, Adam. Three years. Every day at the beginning. Every sodding day. The first year was one long bloody training camp. You've just seen the result: a few metres. That's all. Three years for a few metres. My feet won't walk.'

I nodded. Sat in silence. Waiting for her to continue.

'It's not just about exercise and will power, you know. Though that's what people seem to think. As if you get transformed into some kind of bloody sports fanatic as soon as you end up in a wheelchair. They expect you to struggle and train and then leap up and walk or at least start playing wheelchair hockey and taking part in the Paralympics.'

'That's not what I meant.'

'What people don't understand is that everything depends on what kind of injury it is. There are thousands and thousands of nerves controlling our muscles. Important little threads all over the damned place. It might be a hundredth of a millimetre of some essential nerve that's destroyed or trapped. If you're bloody lucky there might be a minute chance of retraining a muscle. The nerves can even knit together, make a new link. But if so, it occurs in the first couple of years. If nothing happens then, nothing will happen. Ever. Whatever you do.'

'Is that what your doctor said, that there's no hope for you?'

'The doctors don't know. They come and stare at you in their white coats. But they're aware of whether you're making any progress or just standing twitching all day long. They're told by the physiotherapists. They're the ones who do the work. Who nag you. Who ring you at home and scold you if you're shirking or encourage you if you're sitting bawling in a corner because everything looks so hellishly black. It's thanks to them that you keep going.'

'So you haven't given up, then?'

'I don't believe in miracles any more. But I haven't stopped exercising. I have to carry on with physical training, everyone has to. And I'm lucky. My injury's low down in my spine. The higher up it is, the more paralysed you are. But I didn't actually break my back. It's an incomplete spinal cord injury.'

'What does that mean?'

'There's a spinal cord lesion and the nerve is trapped. But I don't think about the injury any more. I want to try and find a new life now, for myself and this chair. Instead of fantasising that one day I'll be able to go out dancing.'

'How often do you exercise, then?'

'Once a week.'

I said nothing. But her answer really infuriated me: once a week! Utterly futile! That was nothing. People who only crap once a week die of constipation. But I bit my tongue.

'I'm sorry,' I said.

'Sorry for what?'

'For not having any idea what you've been through. For asking such daft questions.'

'No, it's good that you are, Adam. Go on asking me daft questions.'

But the question that was burning on my lips like a flame was one that I still didn't ask. The question that had been weighing on me for three years, that kept me awake at night as I lay in bed in a cold sweat whispering, *No, Mary-Lou! No! Don't do it!* I couldn't bring myself to ask it. I swallowed it. Yet over and over again it would rise up into my mouth as a burning question I would douse in saliva. I could feel the words hissing against my tongue before evaporating in steam and vanishing into nothing: *Mary-Lou, did you really jump from the cherry tree?*

But I didn't ask. I didn't dare, Mary-Lou.

I walked down to the jetty, took off my bloodstained clothes and rinsed them in the lake. I reached for the bar of natural soap and the old scrubbing brush hidden in a cavity under the boards. I scrubbed the clothes on one of the jetty boulders and thought the results looked quite promising. Then I spread them out to dry.

I went over to the bench and put on my jeans and blue sweater. They were dry and warm from the sun. I could feel something scraping my back and when I put my hand there I found an envelope sticking out of my pocket. Of course, Mary-Lou's letter! It was rather the worse for wear. Crinkled with damp. The writing smudged.

'Mary-Lou!' I shouted. 'There was a letter for you!'

She appeared in the doorway.

'I forgot it yesterday. It looks as if it's from your mum.'

I smoothed it out as best I could and passed it to her. She examined it, turning it over.

'Did you take it swimming with you?'

'It was in my jeans all night. They were soaked through from the rain yesterday.'

She slit it open with her finger but had trouble unfolding the letter itself because it seemed to have stuck together when it dried.

'It might be best to wet it again,' I said. 'Let me have a go at it.'

I went in and put a pan of water on to boil and held the letter over the steam. The paper quickly softened and I peeled it carefully apart.

Mary-Lou read in silence. Turned it over. Laughed out loud. Then folded it up again.

'She sends you her very best wishes – and Anders,' she added with a giggle.

'My father? Why?'

'Because she thinks he's here, you idiot.'

'What makes her think that?'

'Because that's what I told her, idiot. You don't think she'd have let me come if she'd known I'd be completely alone with you, do you?'

'I'm just going for a little stroll,' I said, holding up my sketchpad and some pencils so she'd think I wanted to do some work in peace and quiet.

'Mmm,' she said without opening her eyes.

She lay on the jetty sunning herself in a black bikini,

116

her dark brown hair falling loosely over the boards. Her body was slender, her breasts quite large. She looked like any normal fifteen-year-old girl. And yet fate had left its mark on her. Her calf muscles were small and flat: you could see she hadn't used them for a long time. You could also see she had used her arm muscles all the more.

She called out after me as I was going.

'Be careful...'

Since I didn't really understand how she meant it I didn't respond. I just paused and nodded, but she didn't see because she still had her eyes closed.

'...that the fox doesn't get you!'

'Very funny,' I shouted back.

I followed the path through the enchanted forest. Walked along noticing all the roots it was now so easy to step over. Kicked at them, as if trying to make them realise they shouldn't be there.

When I got to the Bronze Age I could see the wild strawberries were ripe. Their sweet smell hung in the air along the side of the meadow where they grew most. I breathed it in, remembering the scent from all the previous summers and thinking that if smells were visible, a bright red veil would be fluttering gently in the breeze over the meadow.

I crouched down and took a plastic bag out of my pocket and started picking the firm, snub-nosed berries. They were just like real strawberries, only smaller. Elves' strawberries is what my father used to call them when I was little.

117

I picked a bagful. Then I sat down on the grass and tried some. They tasted better than most wild strawberries. I knew Mary-Lou thought so too.

After Mary-Lou went to bed that night I stayed behind in the kitchen. I sat at the window sketching some swift impressions of the dusk. Aspects of the garden, the jetty and the lake in the last red rays of the setting sun.

When I thought she must have gone to sleep I went to the larder and got three eggs, whisked them, poured in two cups of sugar, whisked a bit more. Added two cups of flour, one cup of milk, folded in the last of the margarine, and sprinkled some vanilla sugar over the top.

When the cake was in the oven I realised I'd forgotten the baking powder. Shrugged my shoulders, whipped some cream. When I took it out it had only risen a few centimetres. I wouldn't be able to cut any flan cases out of it.

I considered the options while I waited for it to cool. Then I spread some raspberry preserve on it and covered the whole concoction with a thick layer of whipped cream. And wrote across the white cream in red letters made of wild strawberries: *Happy Birthday Mary-Lou*.

When I'd finished I put the cake in the larder. I got undressed and crept into bed. Then, when the whole house was absolutely quiet, I heard Mary-Lou's voice in the darkness.

'What was it you were doing, Adam?'

'Nothing.'

'Nothing smells jolly good.'

Silence reigned again for a few minutes. Then I called out, 'Did you shut the hens in?'

''Course.'

Mary-Lou's birthday started well. I woke up early of my own accord and tiptoed out for a pee. I could feel the dewy grass on my bare feet as I stood there thinking through what remained to be done. The situation was under control, except that I'd forgotten to pick any harebells at the Bronze Age. I made up for it now by picking a bouquet of red willowherb. I took the ones growing furthest away, obviously.

I laid the flowers on the ramp while I went down to the jetty to wash. I liked rinsing my face in cold lake water and washing myself with the stone-hard soap that was always scratchy from the sand stuck to it. I brushed my teeth, spitting out a stream of toothpaste froth that floated away on the smooth surface of the water.

You'll have a sunny day for your fifteenth birthday, Mary-Lou, I thought. It seemed a good omen.

I put the water on and took out the cake while I was waiting for it to boil. I found a tray in the cupboard under the sink and covered it with a clean tea towel. I got out two cups, a jar of honey and two plates and teaspoons. I trimmed the willowherb with the bread knife and put them in a tall slim beer glass with the words *Holsteiner Bier* in gold on the side.

Then I poured tea in one cup and coffee in the other, padded over to Mary-Lou's door with the tray and began to sing 'Happy birthday to you'.

As I went into the room it struck me how much more practical it was now that the threshold was gone. Mary-Lou was lying with her face to the wall. She turned slowly and her lips formed a huge grin even before she'd properly woken up.

'Wow, Adam,' she murmured, 'you don't mean to say you've done all this just for me?'

She heaved herself up to a half-sitting position, her eyes going from the tray to me, from me to the tray. I felt rather embarrassed because giving a friend a treat on her fifteenth birthday wasn't exactly going over the top.

'Adam, you're so nice,' she said, laying her tousled head on my lap as I sat beside her on the bed, so that I couldn't resist rumpling her hair.

'And what a brilliant cake you've made!'

'Many happy returns of the day,' I said, stroking her cheek.

'No, not like that. I want a proper birthday kiss,' she said, raising her head.

She closed her eyes and I bent forward and kissed her tentatively on the lips.

'Like that?'

'Much better! There's something special about being fifteen. You're grown up. You can begin to live without a safety net. You can take responsibility and have only yourself to blame when things go wrong. Though I know you've been doing that for yonks.'

'True. But you're right. It's a period of your life that's over for ever and a new one beginning. Childhood has come to an end. Well, it finishes by about twelve, I suppose. But it's much more obvious now. Your guardian angels are getting tired. They have new kids to think about.'

Mary-Lou made no reply and I wondered if she'd misunderstood me. In fact she could have done with her guardian angel staying on. Then her life might have turned out differently.

'Twelve, fifteen and eighteen are the only birthdays you need. They're the only ones I intend to celebrate anyway.'

Mary-Lou nodded. She could hardly tear her eyes away from the tray.

'What super flowers!' she exclaimed as if seeing the fiery red blooms in the beer glass for the first time.

'Rosebay willowherb,' I said. 'The nearest thing to roses the garden has to offer.'

'I've always loved them,' said Mary-Lou.

'I don't know what I think,' I said. 'Britt likes them. She calls them "last chance".'

'Why?'

'Because of that distinctive purplish-red colour. Old women wear colours like that when they want to dress up. To make themselves look good. It's their last chance to get a man. According to Britt.'

Mary-Lou laughed.

'I've never heard that before.'

'I use them as a calendar. When the flowers at the top have come out, the summer holidays are nearly over.'

'Then we'd better take our last chance and enjoy the rest of the summer,' she said.

She inspected the topmost flowers. They were only half out. There was still time. Plenty of time. Summer wasn't over yet.

'So many eyes,' she continued. 'I remember what you said about flowers being the earth's eyes. This must be the best example there is.'

'Yeah.'

'Do you know what we used to call them?'

'What?'

'Poor man's foxgloves!'

We both laughed.

'Would you like a piece of cake? They're genuine wild strawberries, though the rest is a bit of a cheat.'

She nodded and I cut a large slice for her and almost as big a one for myself.

'It's delicious, Adam,' she said, putting a large strawberry to her lips and letting it melt in her mouth. 'Was it these you were picking yesterday afternoon?'

'Yeah.'

We thoroughly enjoyed that cake; it wasn't too bad, despite leaving out the baking powder. Then I thought we were approaching the moment in every birthday when the mind turns to presents.

'I haven't bought you anything,' I said.

'This is better than a present,' she said, pointing at the birthday tray with her teaspoon.

'But I've got something for you anyway.'

'What?'

'It's you yourself who's the present, Mary-Lou. I'm going to give you my image of you. The truest likeness

I can create. But I can only do it with your help. You've got to sit for me. Perhaps for several hours. Will you?'

'Of course I will,' she said, sounding quite touched.

'Do you remember that summer when we were twelve and used to go up to the Bronze Age all the time? You said to me once: "Draw me, Adam!" I didn't want to then. I didn't feel I was good enough. But thinking about it since, I knew I wanted to try when I'd learnt more. I'm ready now.'

'No, I don't actually remember it,' Mary-Lou said pensively, 'but it would be a really cool present to get. It's the best thing you could give me.'

We spent almost all day on the jetty. It was the warmest day so far. The sun was at last getting as hot as it ought to for the time of year. We lay panting and moaning about the heat-wave the way you're meant to when summer finally arrives. It was too hot to do anything, even drawing.

'What do you think you'll do eventually?' Mary-Lou asked. 'Will you be an artist?'

'I don't know. So many people are good at art. If you're going to be an artist you have to develop a style of your own, your own way of seeing things. I don't know whether I ever could.'

'What will you be if you don't become an artist?'

'I thought at one stage it would be fun to be a botanist and have a job involving flowers, but I think it might be best to keep that as a hobby, like my father.'

'So might you be a journalist, like him?'

'Dunno, maybe. Or a photographer. That sounds more fun.'

'You'd make a great photographer, Adam.'

'What about you? You used to want to be a singer when you were little. You gave performances in the barn. Do you remember? I always thought what a lovely voice you had.'

Mary-Lou laughed.

'Well, I still sing. That's probably the only thing about me that's the same. I sing in a choir, as you know. But I stopped dreaming about being a singer long ago. If I'm going to do anything like that, I'd rather be an actor, but there isn't a lot of demand for actors in wheelchairs.'

We were quiet after this. I noticed we were both looking over towards Norden Farm. Or sneaking glances, I should say, because it felt slightly taboo.

'Aren't you in touch with Björn?'

'He phones occasionally. Not as much now as at the beginning. It's quite sweet really. He spends the whole time apologising. He sometimes sounds drunk.'

'You don't want to go and see him?'

Mary-Lou shook her head.

'He doesn't want me to.'

'Why ever not?'

'He's said he doesn't. I think he's ashamed of how he is now.'

'And you don't want to because he doesn't want you to?'

'Something like that.'

Presently we went in the water. I got in first and lifted Mary-Lou down from the jetty and carried her nearer the beach, setting her down on the rippled sandy bottom just where the water came up to my knees. She lay on her back, stretching her body out.

'Oh, it's gorgeous,' she said. 'It's so warm!'

I nodded in agreement and waded out a bit further and plunged in. Then I went and got the board and tried to float on it. But it didn't go very well today. My head kept going under.

'Be more confident, Adam!' she shouted.

When I carried her ashore she held her dripping arms around my neck and gave me a wet kiss right on the mouth.

'Thanks for helping me,' she said. 'That's the first time I've bathed in a real lake. First time in three years. It's a perfect birthday treat.'

That evening we hit on the idea of having a birthday dinner on the jetty. I found the barbecue in the outhouse but it was in a filthy state and it took ages to get rid of all the old charcoal and rust that had solidified into a sort of mulch in the bottom. The grill was covered in soot and burnt-on bits of food. My father was so slovenly. He'd never have got by without me.

'Oh look, here are the sails for the boat,' I said as I shifted some boxes in my hunt for a wire brush.

Mary-Lou wheeled herself forward to see as I extracted the spritsail and laid it on the concrete floor. It was more grey than white and smelt musty.

'It seems to be in one piece, at any rate,' I said.

'Is there a foresail too?'

'I think so.'

I went back to the pile of boxes and dragged out a smaller sail. It stank of mould and was even greyer.

'It doesn't look very attractive but it probably still works,' said Mary-Lou.

'Shall we take the boat out?'

She shook her head.

I hung both sails on the spikes in the side of the outhouse where we used to put the net, so they could dry in the sun.

'I'll give them a good scrub with soap later,' I said.

I lugged out the barbecue and then we searched everywhere for charcoal but there wasn't any. No lighting fluid either.

'We'll use the natural method,' she said. 'Fir cones are just as good.'

I took a plastic bucket and went to the edge of the woods and filled it with cones that were tinder dry. I laid a few dead twigs on top that I broke off from inside the base of a fir tree.

Mary-Lou had put some screwed-up newspaper in the barbecue. I built a wigwam of dry twigs round it and then heaped the cones carefully on the top. I made a little tunnel under the twigs and set light to the paper.

I went into the kitchen and took the roasting pan out of the oven and filled it with vegetables that I'd peeled and cut into fairly large chunks. There were white onions, tomatoes, carrots, potatoes and strips of red pepper. I poured in a tin of mushrooms, salt and pepper and a dash of cooking oil and took it to Mary-Lou.

'It's burning well,' I said and put the pan on the grill over the glowing red-hot cones.

'I'm just going to make a sauce,' I added, heading off to the house again.

I knocked up a quick sauce from a tin of tomatoes and some crème fraîche, rubbing in some of Britt's dried herbs.

Then I went to the larder, past the shelves of tins to the back wall where I knew there would be some wine. I pulled out a bottle of white, selecting the label that appealed to me most.

When I came back fumes were rising from the pan and there was an aroma of food all over the jetty. Mary-Lou was changing. She had taken off her black bikini and was putting on her jeans. The evening sun bathed her face and milk-white breasts in a soft orange glow.

'I've burnt my thighs,' she said, turning to me with a total lack of embarrassment. Her breasts were really pretty and of course I couldn't help looking at them. She giggled, as if only just realising she had no top on, and slipped on a sweater.

'Do you drink wine?' I asked, holding up the bottle that I'd had behind my back.

'Not very often,' she said. 'But it would be fab to have some tonight.'

'It's not very cold,' I said, feeling the bottle with the palm of my hand. 'White wine should be chilled, otherwise it's undrinkable, according to my father.'

'No problem,' said Mary-Lou, taking the bottle from my hand and in a single movement throwing it over her shoulder into the water. There was a big splash and the heavy bottle sank like a stone. We could see it settling on the bottom.

'Clever,' I said with a laugh. 'How's the grub coming on?'

'Nearly ready,' she replied, stirring it with a stick that had been polished smooth by the waves.

'Do we need plates?'

'No, we can dig in straight from the pan. But a fork wouldn't be a bad idea.'

I went indoors again.

'And glasses!' she shouted after me. 'And my flowers!'

I found two unchipped wineglasses in the cupboard, picked up two forks from the dish drainer, the beer-glass vase of willowherb and a corkscrew, plus the remains of Mary-Lou's birthday cake.

It was one of those evenings with loads of mirages on the lake and we amused ourselves trying to outdo each other in all the weird shapes we could count. Everything had kind of lifted itself several metres and was hovering above the water. Stones, trees, jetties, boats and islands, all floating around in front of us. The wine may have had a hand in it too, of course.

I told Mary-Lou I thought I could see part of Paris. The quays along the Seine and a café with red awnings and a long row of those stalls where they sell old books.

'Have you been to Paris?'

'I went with my dad on a job during the winter holidays. Three days.'

'Did you like it?'

'Yeah, though there were too many cars everywhere.'

'What did you do?'

'Oh, we went to Euro-Disney for a few hours, and we saw the Arc de Triomphe and the Eiffel Tower and the Mona Lisa. It's true what your friend said, there is a lift in the Eiffel Tower.'

The pan was now completely empty and lying on the lake-bed by the jetty. We had drunk most of the wine and I would guess we weren't entirely sober. I could detect it in Mary-Lou, who was giggling at nearly everything I said.

'Moaner Lisa,' she said now with a chortle. 'Fancy being called that. Moaner! Moaner Lisa!'

Then she was serious again. Looking out across the lake. She took a long drag on her cigarette and exhaled the smoke slowly to form a pale cloud.

'I don't think I'd like life in Paris. I prefer peace and quiet. I even find Stockholm too much. I'd like things always to be the way they are for us here now, Adam.'

'Your everyday life?' I said, remembering what she'd said recently.

'Yes. Trying to create a world within the world. A world of your own.'

'Like that hermit did on Fjuk.'

'Right. Sort of. But not alone. Definitely not on my own. You've got to have someone to be with. Someone you can depend on. That's not so damned easy.'

I was a bit startled by the sudden hardness in her voice. I didn't say any more. She stubbed out her cigarette on the jetty. The silence drew a heavy line under her words.

The lake was waking up. Ring after ring was appearing and spreading ripples on the dark water. It was beautiful, almost a little magical. I thought I could hear faint gulping sounds. I knew what it was because I'd come across it before. It was fish snapping up insects on the surface.

'It's grayling, isn't it?' I asked Mary-Lou.

She nodded.

'You ought to try and catch some,' she said.

'With nets?'

'With flies,' she said. Then giggled again. 'Or bees,' she said, giggling even more. 'You've got enough here.'

I laughed too. Then abruptly she sat up on the jetty and took off her sweater.

'I want to go in the water, Adam. It's so beautiful. Carry me! Come on!'

She held her arms up in the air.

I stood up.

'Do you want your jeans on?'

'No, you can take them off for me.'

I took hold of the legs and tugged, and when the jeans came off over her heels I lost my balance and tumbled over on the jetty. Mary-Lou broke into a fit of giggles again.

I folded her jeans and put them on the wheelchair.

'I don't need these either,' she said, pulling off her

pants and flinging them aside. 'We ought to go skinny-dipping, that's nicest, isn't it, Adam?'

Her pants had landed on the wine bottle and when she saw them there it brought on a new burst of giggling.

I stripped off too. Then I picked her up, but since I wasn't entirely certain about the effects of the wine I didn't take the risk of climbing in over the stones. I decided to walk along the jetty to the shore and then go in across the beach.

I stepped carefully, watching where I put my feet. The accident of the day before still haunted me. I'd never carried a naked girl before. Mary-Lou's skin felt soft and smooth against mine. That was another reason why I was trying to concentrate on what my feet were doing.

Suddenly there was a cackling up in the garden. Mary-Lou laid her hand on my arm. I stopped, listening.

'There's someone in the garden,' she said, immediately sounding as sober as a judge.

I peered through the trees. Up towards the cottage. I couldn't see anyone.

'It's probably only Britt Börjesson,' I said.

That made Mary-Lou start giggling again. I could feel her warm body kind of quivering in my arms.

I stood still for a minute. There were no more noises to be heard. It was only in American films that things like that happened, I thought. If this had been a film, it would have been exactly the moment for my father and Britt to make their entrance. Just as I was standing there naked with a naked wheelchair-bound girl in my arms and an empty bottle of one of Britt's better wines on the jetty. Though they might not notice that, it occurred to me, draped as it was in Mary-Lou's pants.

I started walking again. It must have been Siv and Ruth arguing about a worm. They sounded like that sometimes. I said as much to Mary-Lou.

'I thought I heard someone anyway,' she insisted.

The water was really warm. I carried her out till it was part way up my thighs. I must have had a vague idea that it would be fun to bathe together. I tried to sit down on the sand with her in my arms, but we toppled over backwards. Mary-Lou was convulsed again and I couldn't help myself from bursting into such a guffaw that we both collapsed in the water.

Then Mary-Lou jerked to one side with a shriek. She'd felt something brush against her back.

'Oh, I thought I felt a fish,' she said.

I didn't say anything. I knew what it was. It was my stiff willy that had touched her. I felt embarrassed and realised she'd guessed what sort of fish it was as well.

Mary-Lou wanted to sleep outside in the open. On the jetty. It seemed a great idea to me so I went in and got some blankets and pillows and made two comfy beds for us. Then I ran over and shut in Siv and Ruth. They seemed to be quite used to their outdoor life already and went in by themselves at night. I couldn't think why we hadn't thought of it before. Now they were already half asleep in the car. I said goodnight.

I returned to Mary-Lou and helped her lie down on the jetty and bedded down beside her. We lay on our backs, my arm underneath her, gazing at the moon that hung like a luminous boomerang over the forest.

It wasn't entirely silent. There was a boat out on the lake, a sailing boat using its engine because of the windless night, I presumed. Now and then the tones of distant music wafted towards us from a party in a summer cottage somewhere inland.

'I love sleeping outdoors,' said Mary-Lou.

'Me too.'

Then we discovered that the sky was full of bats skimming over the water and it felt fabulous to be lying there almost among them. They were swooping around us like little ghosts with their quick bobbing movements. One came so close that Mary-Lou ducked under the blanket.

I saw I'd forgotten to turn the light off in the kitchen. And the door was open. Ah, well, it didn't matter, nothing ever happened here. You could trust people out here.

I said that to Mary-Lou, but got no answer.

I snuggled down beside her, listening to her slow calm breathing. She sounded like the lake. I tried to breathe to her rhythm, and fell asleep.

I slept fitfully. Dreamt a weird dream about being naked in Paris and Britt Börjesson coming up to me. She was also naked and her breasts were swinging heavily with every step she took. She looked at me and laughed. Then she took hold of my willy and tugged at it experimentally a few times. She nodded and gave me an accusatory look. 'What is it?' I asked fearfully. 'Hold out your hands, my son,' she said. I wanted to scream at her that I wasn't her son, that she must be mixing me up with someone else. But not a word would pass my lips. I stood there open-mouthed, like a dead fish. I rubbed my hands over my eyes and they felt like protuberant white balls. I'm a dead fish, I thought, feeling my panic growing. 'Well, my son,' said Britt and I could defend myself no longer. I felt her wrapping her arms around me and lifting me up. She was carrying me off. 'No!' I cried. 'Put me down!' Then I caught sight of Björn. Right beside us. He was fully dressed and wearing his grey cap pushed back on his forehead. He was grinning at me. 'Speak French, lad, so she can understand what you're saying.'

I woke with a start, at first under the impression I'd only been asleep for a little while. But it was light. The sun was up. It had just risen above the treetops on the opposite peninsula and was shining on our side of the bay. On the other side the water was as black as the granite beneath Mary-Lou's cherry tree. A gull was wailing on the jetty. Mary-Lou moved uneasily under the blanket. The gull rose and flew off in agitation over the lake.

'What is it?' she mumbled.

'Only a gull.'

I looked around. Saw the empty wine bottle and two half-empty glasses. Some clothes scattered about on the jetty. A beer glass with red flowers in. Two stubbed-out cigarette ends. I could feel a slight headache and wondered whether it was because of the wine or the hard boards beneath us.

I dragged myself up, pulled on my jeans and went in to get the toothpaste and brushes. Mary-Lou was awake when I got back. She was lying under her blanket watching me. I rinsed one of the glasses, filled it with water and put it next to her on the jetty. I squeezed some toothpaste on to her brush and gave it to her. She put it in the glass.

'The toothpaste will fall off,' I said.

Mary-Lou looked at the glass and nodded.

'Yes, Mummy,' she said.

I rinsed my face several times to wash away the last traces of my unpleasant dream. When I'd cleaned my teeth I looked at Mary-Lou. She was still under the blanket.

'I'm going in to fix some breakfast,' I said.

As I walked up to the house I was thinking she was right: I did feel like a bloody mother.

Afterwards, Mary-Lou wanted to sit for me.

'Draw me now, Adam!' she said with a soft voice of authority which I found difficult to resist.

I could have wished for a better day to start my tricky task.

'We could have a shot at it, I suppose,' I said without great enthusiasm.

'What fun! Where do you want me to sit?'

I'd thought a lot about how I would do the portrait of Mary-Lou. Whether to draw her in context or just sketch her face. My first idea was to do it up at the Bronze Age because I had a notion that that was where it all began. But I could see that wouldn't be possible.

'Maybe here on the jetty,' I suggested.

'In the wheelchair?'

I considered for a moment. I'd intended it to be without the chair. Now I wasn't sure why. Wouldn't it be a falsification, trying to improve her image? Or shouldn't Mary-Lou herself be the focus of interest, not whether she was sitting in a wheelchair? I decided the chair belonged to the picture of her in some way.

'We can try it,' I said. 'At the end. By the boat.'

Mary-Lou rolled along, turning to say, 'I want the flowers in.'

I shook my head.

'It won't look right, Mary-Lou. They'll just seem out of place.'

'I want them anyway.'

'Why?'

'Because they'll be a reminder of yesterday. It was the best birthday of my life.'

'It won't work.'

'Just a few. You're really good at flowers.'

She extracted some of the willowherb from the beer glass and put them in the empty wine bottle. Then held it in her lap.

'Like this,' she said. 'Then you can get it all in.'

I laughed and shrugged.

'Okay, have it your own way, for the time being.'

I went in and got my sketchpad and a 3B pencil. I brought a kitchen stool out because I wanted to be on the same level as Mary-Lou.

'This is so exciting,' she said.

I put the stool a few metres away from her and sat down on it. I looked at her. Screwed up my eyes, opened them slowly. Checked the background, the boat gurgling at the jetty, the smooth shining lake, and in the distance the northern point on the other side. I scratched my forehead with the pencil. It would have been better if she'd been sitting in the garden, maybe under one of the trees, to give a softer light. Out here the sun was like a floodlight.

'It won't be any good,' I said.

'Why not?'

'The sun's too harsh. It flattens everything.'

'On the beach then,' she said, pointing with her foot.

I turned and saw the alder trees. The light seemed more subtle under them.

'Yeah, let's try there,' I said.

I placed her beneath one of the trees and positioned the wheelchair so that the boat was in the view. Then I fetched my stool and sat at a few metres distance.

'This is much better,' I said happily, because the light was quite different. Mary-Lou's face took on colour and life.

'Good,' she said.

I sat for a long time trying to see her. Screwing up my eyes again, opening them. Assessing the contrasts between light and dark. I could feel myself getting nervous. I'd drawn people before, but not like this. It had just been rough sketches of classmates. Now I wanted to do something more. The real Mary-Lou was what I wanted to capture with my pencil. The reality behind the brown eyes. The real reason she jumped out of the cherry tree one July day three years ago.

I tore half a page from the sketchpad and folded it in four. Cut a square hole in the centre. I opened it flat and scrutinised her through the hole.

I turned it this way and that and marked approximately where Mary-Lou should be and how the background would fit. She was watching me with wonderment but said nothing.

And so my hand set to work. I outlined the positions of her head and body, the wheelchair and her right arm on the armrest, pencilled in a few lines across the picture to indicate the background features.

'Am I okay sitting like this?' she asked.

I nodded, lifted my hand, undecided what to do about the flowers in the wine bottle. I hoped they would soon start to droop and be forgotten. But to be on the safe side I sketched them into the picture.

I think we sat there for nearly an hour. Me on my kitchen stool and Mary-Lou in her wheelchair, my pencil swishing across the paper. Whenever I rested for a moment I picked up the viewing frame to examine her. She spoke from time to time. I mostly just nodded in reply. A group of blokes were water-skiing out in the bay but I only noticed them as a vague impression. I inspected my efforts. The shape of Mary-Lou was there now. I could feel it was her I was working on. I felt pleased with myself. But where the face should have been was just an oval ring. All the details remained to be done. I wanted to wait, to proceed carefully, let the picture grow out of me. I'd never drawn so slowly before.

'That's enough for today,' I said, stretching my limbs.

I made a jug of cold lemonade and we drank several glasses in silence. Neither of us was hungry. It was just as hot as yesterday, the sun hanging over us like a ball of fire. I could feel I was wet under my T-shirt, even though all I'd been doing was drawing. Mary-Lou's thighs were burning. She tried my viewing frame and I helped her direct it at various objects. She laughed in delight and said how different it made everything appear. That it was almost like looking at paintings.

I pushed her up to the garden and fetched her book. She sat under one of the apple trees and started reading.

I felt restless and dragged the spritsail down to the beach and out into the water to let it float. When I went back up to get the foresail I saw that she had fallen asleep in her chair. The book had slipped down and was lying open on the grass. I retrieved it, closed it and stuffed it in beside her.

I let the sails drift around in the water for a while. Then I hauled one of them on to the jetty and started scrubbing it with soap. It was a more strenuous job than I'd anticipated, and the sweat was pouring off my brow and down on to my scrubbing-brush hand.

I took a break after the first sail and went into the water with it as I rinsed the soap off. Then I folded it up in the water and heaved the formless bundle over to the wall of the outhouse.

'Aren't you going to practise swimming today?' asked Mary-Lou.

'Later, maybe. After I've cleaned the other sail. Did you sleep long?'

'Only a few minutes.'

'I've got to mow the lawn too. It grows like crazy.'

I ran my foot over the grass. 'If I'm going to use the hand mower it shouldn't be any higher than that. It'll end up looking like a golf course.'

'That would suit me all right,' said Mary-Lou.

I swam with the polystyrene board again that evening. Mary-Lou sat watching me from the jetty. She had her black bikini on and a sweater draped over her thighs.

I lay on my stomach doing arm strokes but after only two or three I could feel my head sinking and had to get up fast.

'It's no good. This board's useless.'

'It's only because you're scared, Adam. You'll see.'

She swung round and wheeled herself swiftly to the other end of the jetty and on to the beach, threw her sweater down on the sand and drove her chair out into the water.

'Come in closer,' she called.

I splashed towards her pushing my board ahead of me.

'Right,' she said, 'that'll do. Give me a hand with the chair.'

I did as she said, positioned it better for her.

'Fine. Now, if you lie down on the board the way you normally do I'll hold it so it keeps steady.'

I didn't think it would work but went along with it to stop her making a fuss. I tried a few strokes and was about to stand up again when I noticed that the board was still firmly under me. I wasn't sinking.

'That's super! Keep going! Keep going!'

I did some more strokes, but then I could feel myself beginning to sink and had to get my feet down quickly.

'Fantastic!' she said. 'Couldn't you feel that the board will stay put? You can't sink, Adam. No way. Give it another go.'

I got back on the board, and tried some more.

'Slow down,' she said.

I made an effort to control my rhythm.

'One...' she counted, 'and two...and three...and four...'

Then I had to stand up again.

'You're doing really well, Adam.'

'No, it's hopeless,' I replied.

Fine weather continuing. 29° and no wind today. Two eggs again. Ruth and Siv enjoying their freedom. Adam will soon be able to swim. We're having a marvellous time!

Mary-Lou had taken over the weather diary. She was writing while I prepared the grub. She read out what she'd written. I wondered what my dad would think when he read it.

That bit about me being able to swim soon was far from the truth. There was no way I would ever learn to swim. I could tell when I lay on the board. I just went into a panic. It was no help having Mary-Lou sitting there holding on to me. Nothing helped.

I walked up to the Bronze Age after lunch when Mary-Lou wanted to sit and write in her room. I went on drawing flowers. I'd filled half a notebook already and there was a vague idea taking shape in my mind that I might eventually be able to do every plant on my dad's inventory. We could turn it into a real flower manual, *Flowers of the Bronze Age* by Anders and Adam O. What if my father could get his act together and write a text for it, about the meadow and its plants, about the old names of the flowers and what they were once used for? He'd be able to look it all up in any number of reference books.

This was how John Bauer started off. He was always out in the countryside, sketching flowers. Training himself to observe. When he eventually became a real artist, he painted a soul into nature. The forest came alive in his hands. Where there had been dead stones and moss and old tree stumps, trolls and princesses appeared.

When I got back I could see Mary-Lou down in the garden making strange movements. I wondered what she was doing at first but then I guessed it must be the exercises she'd mentioned, and it struck me that this was the first time she'd done them since she came here. Though I suppose she might have been doing them in her room in the evenings.

I stopped and watched her. She was doing her pelvic and leg exercises. It looked complicated. Then she saw me and waved. I went over and showed her my drawing of a bird's-foot trefoil, which I was quite pleased with, and told her about my idea for a flower book.

'That would be brilliant, Adam,' she said. 'Producing a book together. About our meadow!'

'Was that your exercise programme you were doing?'

'Part of it.'

'Isn't it hard doing it on your own?'

'It's okay.'

'I could help if you want.'

I was about to go on to say that I'd trained the junior indoor hockey team for several seasons and that I'd been solely responsible this last year. That I'd even been on a week's instructor course. But she shook her head.

'There's no need, Adam. It's only little things I have to do to save myself from totally rusting up. So I can get out of the chair. I'm not intending to go in for the Paralympics, as I've already said.'

'Right. I'm off to the shop. Can you think of anything we need?'

'There's a list in the kitchen.'

When I got to the supermarket I went over to the wall where they had leisure items. There were cool-bags, bowls, barbecues, cheap fishing tackle, stuff like that.

I hunted around for a while and then went and asked Linda if they had any water-wings. She seemed pleased to see me.

'We did have some,' she said.

She looked on the shelves and then disappeared out to the store at the back and returned with a cardboard box.

'This is all we've got left,' she said, pulling out two yellow ones.

'They're a bit small.'

She read the label, 'For child up to eight years.'

'No good,' I said. 'I need them for someone bigger.'

Mary-Lou sat for me again in the evening. The willow-herb was drooping but she still insisted on having it there. She said she would pick some more when it died.

I gave in, thinking of the portrait John Bauer did of his wife. Her name was Esther and she was an artist too. He painted her in a summer meadow against a background of silver birches with a lily of the valley in her frock.

Mary-Lou wanted to see how I was progressing but I stuck to my guns and refused to let her see it before it was finished.

'Do you have to be so secretive?' she said sullenly.

I didn't reply but started measuring up the proportions so I could carry on where I'd left off. I went on with her hair. It fell straight down to a level with her chin and then curled in towards her neck. Last time, after the night on the jetty, she had just run her fingers through it. It was full of life then, it had a vitality in it that I liked. Now she'd combed it and it hung like a limp curtain.

'Could you tilt your head up a fraction?' I asked.

'Like this?'

'That's perfect.'

To draw you I must know you, I thought. I measured the distance between her roughed-in eyes and her chin. Then I laid my pencil across the paper and marked where her left ear should come.

I felt that every detail I attempted, every line I drew, every shadow I added, raised a question. A question that had something to do with her. Or with her and me.

What did we know about each other? What did we want to know? Should we keep some things to ourselves? What we were ashamed of, the darker side? Or should we reveal our souls to those who wanted to know? Dredge up all the crap from deep down inside?

Or – does it vary? Are all human beings different, some very open and some very closed? I was both, depending on who I was with and what mood I was in.

'How's it going?' Mary-Lou asked.

'All right,' I said. 'Now begins the awkward part.'

'I feel like Mona Lisa,' she said with an introspective smile.

'You're much prettier.'

'Is it true that she was a man?'

'Who? Mona Lisa?'

'Yes. I heard someone say that.'

'I don't think so,' I said. 'Leonardo da Vinci was a genius. He lived in the fifteenth century yet he painted better that we do today.'

'I wonder who she was.'

I let that pass. Thought instead: And what about you, Mary-Lou? Who are you, actually? I don't really know you at all.

Maybe it was my own fault. Maybe I had the wrong picture of you in my mind. Maybe it was just that memory of the summer when we were twelve that haunted me all the time. Were we really the same people at fifteen that

145

we had been when we were twelve? I posed the question to myself and came up with the answer: no.

You move on. All the time. Onward and forward. I had to try and see the Mary-Lou who was in front of me here and now.

'You're holding the flowers over your face again,' I said.

'Sorry.'

I didn't want to do any more. She was wooden today. It wasn't just her hair. It was the whole of her. She was sitting in her chair like a china doll.

'I think we'll stop. The light's all wrong,' I lied.

I got out Britt's lawnmower. It was still boxed up in its original packaging, the handle separately covered in bubble wrap. Britt was so finicky. I could never understand how she could share a house with my father.

I lifted the mower out and screwed on the handle. It was just like new. Painted blue with the words *Gardena 5000* in white on the metal blade-cover.

'Wait, I want to help!' Mary-Lou shouted as I rolled it out into the garden.

I gave her the mower and she took a firm grip on the handle. I went behind pushing the wheelchair. The little mower purred like a kitten as it ate up the grass.

'Doesn't it cut well?' she cried.

I merely grunted, because it was taking all my strength to steer both her and the mower between the trees by the outhouse. Then we set off straight down the middle of the garden. Siv and Ruth came scampering along behind us. They liked short grass too. Mary-Lou saw them and laughed. She was in a cheerful mood.

'Let's sing something, Adam!'

'What?'

She started on John Lennon's 'Imagine'. And though I was no good at singing, I joined in too. It felt okay doing it with her, because her voice drowned out mine. She was a fantastic singer. A powerful voice and totally clear. As we were about to turn at the stone border below the privy I paused for a minute. The mower fell silent. I stopped singing to concentrate on the wheelchair. But Mary-Lou's voice went on, right across the garden, out across the lake, 'Imagine there's no heaven, it isn't hard to do . . . '

It was so beautiful it made me shiver.

Then I set the mower to work again, as backing instrument.

Mary-Lou wanted us to put in some more swimming practice, but I'd had enough. It was pointless. I didn't want to. I said I'd get by without being able to swim. I'd buy myself a new lifejacket instead. You could get ordinary jackets with lifejackets sewn in the lining. That's what I'd have.

'How childish you are,' she said forcefully. 'I thought you were more mature than that.'

'What do you mean? It's up to me. Not everyone can swim. Not everyone can drive. There's nothing odd about it.'

'I don't give a damn about driving. There's always

147

trains and buses. They're better for the environment anyway. But you have to be able to swim. Come on!'

'No.'

'Stop arguing and come and practise,' she ordered.

'I'll decide for myself whether to or not. You don't want me to help you with your exercises. I've accepted that. You'll just have to accept that I don't want to.'

I was pleased to have thought of that argument. She'd have trouble getting round that. And it did indeed shut her up. She sat on the jetty for a long time sulking or thinking. I wasn't sure which.

But she wasn't one to give up at the first hurdle.

'Does it mean so much to you?'

'What?'

'Whether you help me with my stretching exercises?'

'I wanted to for your sake, Mary-Lou.'

'It's for your sake that I want you to learn to swim.'

Silence. She scowled at me.

'And if I let you?'

'Give you some training?'

'Yes. Will you try to swim then?'

I'd fallen into her trap. I didn't want to. The last time I'd tried I felt a fear I couldn't cope with. The very thought of polystyrene had begun to make me feel ill.

'I don't know.'

'It would be only fair, wouldn't it?'

'It's much worse for me in the water. You don't run any risk of drowning.'

'You're scared, that's why.'

I didn't say anything. Tried to think of an excuse. I

had a hundred reasons for not going into the water. But then I realised there wasn't much point in lying about it any more. I looked out over the lake and thought I could see a shoal of grayling lurking in the bay again. I shrugged.

'I don't much like the feel of it,' I admitted.

'Let's practise leg strokes instead. You can hold on to my wheelchair, then your head will never go under.'

I thought about it. Leg strokes didn't sound too dangerous. 'Then can I help you afterwards?'

She nodded.

'All right. But only leg strokes,' I agreed.

I pushed her chair into the water. The recent fine weather had warmed it up considerably. At least close in to the shore. I knew from experience that it could change back equally fast. It only needed the wind to shift and it would drive the warm surface water straight out again. One summer when I was little I lost an inflatable whale because of that: I'd been playing with it and had just run across to the trees on the beach to have a pee and when I turned round it was way out on the lake. I screamed of course and Dad came running down from the garden. He swam after it but it was no use. The whale was faster. 'It'll probably blow over to Fjuk,' said Britt merrily when Dad came swimming back to the jetty.

'Come on then,' said Mary-Lou.

I lay straight out in the water holding tight to one of the wheels of the wheelchair and started doing some leg movements. I'd practised some on the jetty earlier under Mary-Lou's guidance so I knew they were quite good.

'That's fine,' she said. 'Make your legs stretch in a straight line at the end of each one.'

'This isn't so bad,' I said.

'You see?'

We kept it up for a good while, until she said it was enough.

'You do the best leg strokes in the world, Adam.'

But when I said it was her turn to practise leg strokes she didn't want to.

'I've already done my schedule for today.'

'Do you do it every day? I thought you said once a week.'

'Well, I'm supposed to do it frequently, but I don't always.'

'Why not?'

'Because I don't feel like it.'

We went indoors instead. I'd bought a big loaf and we made hardboiled egg sandwiches with dill-flavoured caviar, on special offer. I'd got out a packet of drinking chocolate that I'd found in the kitchen cupboard.

'Do you sing that in the choir?' I asked as I poured steaming hot chocolate into her cup.

'"Imagine"? Yes, occasionally. We sang it in St Catherine's Church. You know, the one that burnt down and was rebuilt. It was the best feeling in the world singing there. I thought the roof was going to lift off.'

'Pity I didn't know about it,' I said.

We talked about going fishing for grayling one evening. The only problem was we didn't have any flies.

Mary-Lou said that Björn used to fish on the lake when she was little. He had a long pole sticking out from the boat with lines trailing in the water. Every line had artificial flies on. I said I could remember it.

'Wasn't there any fishing tackle to go with the boat when you bought this cottage?' she asked.

'Not that I know of. Though it's a long while ago. I'll have a hunt in the outhouse. I was going to look for the mast anyway.'

I picked up my pad of flower sketches and started writing in the names, the Swedish first and then adding the Latin in brackets from my father's flower handbook. Mary-Lou sat watching me.

'You didn't think I sat well today, did you? That was why you stopped.'

'No, it wasn't that. It didn't feel right, somehow.'

'What didn't?'

'Everything. It was the wrong light, and you had your hair all freshly combed and were too self-aware. The first time you just sat there like your natural self. You looked really good. Real cool. Today you were Mona Lisa.'

'You could have said something,' she muttered.

I went on searching in the flower book for a cinquefoil I wasn't sure about.

'Did you check to see if there was any post?' she asked.

'No, I forgot. I'll go tomorrow.'

I'd promised Dad I would clean out the chicken coop, and I made an early start on it the next morning. The grass was still covered in dew. I released Siv and Ruth from their quarters and threw some corn on the ground in the chicken run. Then I inspected the interior of the car. There was a centimetre-thick layer of droppings on the floor. I chipped into it at random with a screwdriver. It was dry and hard, as if it had been baked on.

I wondered how best to attack it. I fetched a spade and a bucket from the outhouse. The dung formed a complete mat-like covering and when I managed to get the spade under it, it lifted in large slices. I really needed the wheelbarrow, but I didn't dare put chicken shit in that.

Siv and Ruth stood there watching me, as if anxious about what might happen next. Then they shook themselves and traipsed out into the garden.

When the sun came up over the point it got as hot as an oven in the car. I was on my knees stripped to the waist shovelling chicken shit with sweat pouring off me.

Having cleared the floor of the luggage-space I went and got the soap from under the jetty and a bucket of warm water from the kitchen and set to with the scrubbing brush. The result wasn't perfect but it was considerably cleaner and the car smelt much better. I hoped the hens would think so too.

It was worse in the seating area. There wasn't so much excrement there, but what there was was spread out. The seats were difficult to get clean, though beating them got rid of most of it, and I only had to take the rubber floor mats out and knock the dung off them. I gave the mats and dashboard and windows a good scrub and left the doors open.

Then I went down to the shore and took off my jeans. I soaped my whole body with the scratchy soap and ran out and took a dip in the lake. Seeing that I still wasn't clean I went through the whole procedure a second time.

Mary-Lou was sitting in the kitchen reading the back cover of a novel she'd found on my father's bookshelves.

'God, you stink,' she said, looking up.

I stood on one leg and attempted to crow like a cockerel. But she already had her head in the book again. I made myself some sandwiches and ate standing up.

'We'll do your exercises in a minute,' I said.

Rather reluctantly she let me wheel her out into the garden. I put her in the shade of one of the apple trees and asked her to show me the exercises she normally did.

'They're all different, depending which part of the body you mean.'

'Legs.'

'I have to do a lot of cycling movements. On my back.'

I thought about it.

'Do you think you can do this?' I said, lifting one of her legs forward and about ten centimetres off the ground before lowering it again.

'Do I really have to?' she asked.

'Yes.'

She sighed and got out of the chair. She supported herself by clutching at the tree.

153

'Swing your leg up and down.'

'How many times?'

'At least ten with each leg.'

'Ten each way?'

I nodded.

'Do the right leg first,' I instructed briskly.

She gave me a look of distaste.

'Up!' I said.

She raised her leg slowly. When it was ten centimetres off the ground I quickly interjected, 'A bit more!'

Her leg hesitated for a moment. Then edged up another few centimetres.

'Good! Hold it there!'

But she wouldn't. Her leg came back down. I made no comment.

'Now let's do the left. Up!'

Her left leg started moving.

'Go on,' I said. 'Higher! That's right! And the last little bit! Good. Keep it there for a few seconds if you can.'

Down went the leg again. She was glowering at me.

'That was good,' I said. 'Now the right leg once more.'

A pause, as if she was debating whether to make the effort or not. Then her right foot rose from the grass and her leg started to swing very slowly upwards.

'Come on, a bit higher!'

The leg went on up. I thought it might be just a bit higher than the first time.

'Very good, Mary-Lou! Hold it there if you can.'

The leg stayed in mid-air. I counted silently.

'And down.'

Her foot went back on to the grass.

'Do you think it's hard?' I asked.

'No, just depressing,' she replied.

I laughed.

I didn't know anything about exercises for the handicapped, but the few minutes I'd been working with Mary-Lou made me suspect that she had greater resources than she was demonstrating. I thought she could have got more out of these movements. If she only wanted to. I wondered whether she was being lazy.

I couldn't help thinking of the little Polish guy, Krzysztof, who turned up in the junior team last year. He was as fast as a hare on the pitch but his arm muscles were so undeveloped that he would drop the hockey stick if you so much as looked at him. I gave him a pair of dumbbells and spent a few extra minutes with him each time to see that he was doing it right. Praised him to the skies. Said he could practise at home on his own if he felt like it. Last spring he was declared top goalscorer. He was virtually unstoppable. And at his age I'd been exactly the same at the beginning. Hopelessly weak. I suspect that was the reason I made a special effort for him. Or was it just my motherly instincts?

Every muscle is full of possibilities. It can be developed incredibly if it's exercised properly. And if training is regular. That's the secret. A quarter of an hour a day is nearly two hours a week. A hundred hours a year. As far as I could see there was no difference between Mary-Lou and my seven-year-olds. What can be done, can. What can't, can't. But she'd got her legs moving. I wanted them to move some more.

'Left leg again!' I ordered.

Mary-Lou was sitting for me and I was leaning back in my chair with the sketchpad on my lap drawing carefully on the soft paper. I was beginning to understand why artists use easels. I needed to lay my pad down now, stand away from it, put my head on one side, seek a little inspiration.

She was looking at me out of the corner of her eye. I could see she was thinking about me. Her eyes gave it away. They had a dubious expression. As if she too had taken a few steps back from Adam. Maybe it was because of the exercises. Or it might be this particular situation she wasn't really happy with.

I was almost certain she wasn't aware that I could see what she was thinking. The more I studied her face the more I could read in it.

Our faces are like books. You just have to read them thoroughly. Everything is there. Our whole lives are reflected there. All the tragedies and all the joys we've lived through are etched on them. In the eyes, the lines around the mouth, the angle of the head and chin. That was what I was trying to capture. But I could see several Mary-Lous. Maybe I would have to select just one?

However, drawing is so much more than just making your own version of something. So much you have to know, so much technique, so much practice. Just giving some depth to Mary-Lou's head, to make it stand out from the flat paper, seemed almost impossible.

I was trying to do it with egg-shapes. Drawing a big oval egg and then filling in with more lines through the oval till I thought I could feel the space inside her head.

She was better today than when she was Mona Lisa, but I wasn't happy about her. Her eyes weren't the ones I wanted. Her cheeks were taut, her lips set.

I was working on her right arm that was resting on the arm of the chair. My first sketch of her hand must have been quite good, because I could see it was shaping up well, the fingers flowing out naturally. Hands can be hopeless. Look around you, Gunilla Fahlander used to say, read comics, go to exhibitions. Bad artists never draw hands. They hide them behind backs or patting a dog.

I contemplated her upper arm. Now with clothes on it wasn't apparent how well-developed her upper body was. But having seen her in her bikini – and without her bikini for that matter – I knew her arm muscles were like a weightlifter's.

I skipped her other arm that was holding the wine bottle of willowherb and went on to her legs and feet. She was barefoot today and I liked that, despite the fact that toes were just as difficult as fingers. Her toes were actually quite like fingers. They were long and crooked and intertwined like new-born kittens.

But the pair of bare feet sticking out of the jeans were right. That was Mary-Lou. That was something, I thought, and straightened up.

'That'll do for the time being, I think.'

'I suppose I can't look now either?'

'You know very well you can't.'

The heat-wave continued. We hardly bothered to do anything. We spent all our time on the jetty during the day. We took out more and more stuff and the jetty began to look like a living room. We had a flower-patterned thermos flask, cups, plates, comics strewn about, my old stereo radio, towels, a folding blue plastic chair, a bottle of sun-tan lotion that I'd bought for Mary-Lou at the local supermarket, my sketchpad and a pile of pencils, my dad's flower book and lots of other bits and pieces.

I was half listening to a radio programme about a doctor who'd worked with the mentally ill. Mary-Lou was reading *A Burnt Child* by Stig Dagerman that my dad had bought in a book sale last winter. She was totally immersed in it. Scarcely answered when I spoke. Just licked her finger to turn a page now and then. Late in the afternoon she closed the book with a bang.

'What a good book. Horrible, but good, even though it's so old.'

'Dad thought so too.'

'Have you read it?'

'Not that one. But another one by him. I did an essay on him at school. He committed suicide by gassing himself with the exhaust of his car when he was thirty.'

'Gross,' said Mary-Lou. 'I suppose you could almost tell from the book. It's in the atmosphere. The main

158

character makes a horrific suicide attempt out on an island.'

I knew I had no desire to discuss suicide.

'Shall we go in the water?' I suggested.

'If we can drag ourselves that far,' she said.

That's how it was in this hot weather. That's how brilliant it was.

When evening came and the heat abated I took another exercise session with Mary-Lou on the jetty, the same again, raising the lower leg, though I didn't think it was particularly useful.

She wasn't in the least enthusiastic but she did what I said. Unwillingly and apathetically, as if it had nothing to do with her at all. As if she was only doing it for my sake.

'Hold your leg there,' I said. 'Good! And down . . . '

She gave me a malevolent look, half hidden by her hair which she made no attempt to brush back.

'Left leg up! Good. Go on! Go on! Go on! Force yourself now. Clench your teeth. A bit more. Well done. Hold it there! Good. And down . . . '

I ignored her sullenness. I was concentrating entirely on her legs. I noted everything they did, every little change. I saw she could do it. That there was more to be got out of her. I wondered how much. I had other exercises I thought might suit her. But this wasn't the moment to mention them. It was too soon.

'And the right, up!'

We did ten with each leg, and I praised her lavishly

afterwards. I asked again about her own exercises and she described a few but said she thought they were a complete waste of effort.

'Do you practise walking too?'

'Sometimes.'

'Do you feel like having a go now?'

She shook her head, but I stood up close to her and put my arm round her waist.

'We could try taking just one or two steps,' I said. 'I'd quite like to see what you can do.'

She made no reply. But I could feel her body saying no.

'Then I'll do some arm stroke swimming afterwards. Lots!'

I don't know what she found so fascinating about me learning to swim, but she'd obviously got it into her head that she wanted to teach me. She gave a nod.

'Okay.'

She adjusted her clothes and then I could feel her bracing herself, with a tense jerk through her whole body. She held my hands, squeezing them tight. Then she drew her right foot slowly across the jetty. Stopped. Rested. Concentrated again. Then her left foot made the same stiff movement. We'd travelled a few centimetres. I could feel her bracing herself again. Her hands gripping mine. Her right foot sliding forward. Another pause, more concentration, and then the left foot followed. She was breathing heavily. I could see what a strain it was for her.

'Good,' I said softly so as not to put her off.

She set her body to work some more. I could feel the whole of her involved, every muscle, every nerve doing its bit to help her achieve something that we all do without even giving it a thought, moving our feet a few pathetic centimetres.

I was clasping her round the shoulders now, as if that would help. I could see it was a matter of concentration. It was the brain that was sorting it out. It was her will power making her feet shuffle painstakingly across the jetty.

We'd actually come quite a way now. Much further than I'd thought. If she could manage a bit more we might make the whole length of the jetty. It seemed stupendous that a lame girl could actually walk.

'Brilliant, Mary-Lou!' I whispered. 'This is ace!'

I don't know whether it was my choice of words. But something broke the spell. She lost her concentration. She came to a halt, wobbled and would have fallen if I hadn't been supporting her. She glared at me.

'Just leave me alone.'

'What do you mean?'

'You think you're Jesus Christ, don't you? You think you can train me so I don't have to use that damned chair ever again. You imagine I'll soon be trotting around like everyone else, thanks to you.'

I just stared at her, at a loss for words.

'I'm only trying to help you, Mary-Lou.'

'You shouldn't give a shit about me. Don't you get it? Let me go to hell!'

'No, I can't do that.'

'You're so stupid, Adam. A stupid bloody sports freak is all you are.'

'I care about you. Is that stupid?'

'You don't understand anything. I get so bloody tired of you sometimes.'

She hit out with her arm right across my stomach and at the same time her foot slipped to one side and kicked one of my 3B pencils into the lake.

'Get me my chair, can't you?'

I slunk off along the jetty. But I couldn't help measuring out the distance. One ... two ... three ... and a half. Three and a half metres she'd walked. I thought that was sensational and told her so as she sat down in the chair.

'For God's sake, don't you ever give up!' she screeched and wheeled herself off up the garden.

I stood there watching her go. It was our second real quarrel.

I took the opportunity to draw her again later. She looked fantastic, completely laid-back, her face as tranquil as an island in the sun after a storm. Her eyes radiated calm; no scowling, no frowning. Every muscle had relaxed. Her mouth had a contented expression and her dimples looked like two spiders tattooed on her cheeks. Her hair was hanging naturally and straggly. She was exactly the way I liked her. My pencil was scratching away eagerly. Trying to preserve what my eyes were seeing. If I could only reproduce a little of this, I would never have a bad word to say about artists again. I drew till I got cramp in my fingers. I had no idea how long we'd been sitting there. When I stood up with the sketchpad in my hand one of my feet had gone to sleep. It tingled when I tried to rub it back to life.

'You were bloody good today,' I said.

I could see she wanted to be alone after that, so I suggested she might like to check whether there was any post, because I still hadn't remembered to look.

Her eyes lit up at the suggestion and when she wheeled herself off through the garden I went down to the water again. I jumped in and practised the finest leg strokes in the world.

I hung on to the jetty and worked my legs. It was a pity you couldn't do arm strokes the same way. But even my arm strokes had improved. Mary-Lou said I could swim back and front now. I'd done it a few times with the board under my stomach. Arms and legs at the same time.

But the thought that you were supposed to do it without the board filled me with terror. I was sure I would sink the moment I tried.

When she came back I was sitting on the jetty getting a splinter out of my thumb.

'You're going to have visitors,' she said, and held up a postcard.

'Who's it from?'

'You can read it yourself,' she said, handing it to me. Her voice sounded strange so I took the card and glanced at it quickly. It was a picture of the Palace in Stockholm and I knew immediately it was from my father because that was his type of humour. I skimmed through the short message.

Hi, Son! Hope you're enjoying yourself. It's hot as hell in town. Britt & I are coming out for the weekend. Hope that's OK. We're taking a few days off, so if the weather continues fine we might stay till the middle of next week. Make hay while the sun shines. We'll buy some food in town before we set off. See you Friday evening. Anders.

I was completely knocked for six by the card. Now what? Dad and Britt coming? For the best part of a week!

'What day is it today?' I asked Mary-Lou.

'No idea. Wednesday, maybe.'

Then I remembered I'd heard a rock programme on the radio yesterday that was broadcast on Wednesdays.

'No, it must be Thursday,' I said.

'So it's tomorrow they're coming?'

'I presume so.'

I looked at the card again. Dad hadn't dated it and the postmark wasn't legible. It could have been in the box for several days. *Hi, Son!* Bloody Father!

Neither of us said anything for some time but we must both have been thinking feverishly.

It was extraordinary, I thought, how one little postcard could alter so much. Everything we had built up was suddenly under threat. Our peaceful days chilling out on the jetty. Our lovely mornings with tea and coffee and sandwiches, the long warm evenings as the sun set and the lake went to sleep. The punctual trips in Adam's barrow to the bee house. Routines we had so patiently devised. Or that had developed.

All this was going to change. Carrying on the swimming lessons with Britt and my father here was out of the question. The same applied to Mary-Lou's portrait.

Our world within the world had collapsed.

'What shall we do now, then?' Mary-Lou asked.

'I'll make a sandwich,' I said.

I'd intended making pasta with smoked whitefish because Linda had let me buy half a whitefish cheap in the supermarket. But that was totally impossible now. The evening was ruined. Everything was spoilt. That was how it felt anyway. We couldn't think of anything except that card. In fact we couldn't think at all. Mary-Lou was smoking indoors, even though she knew I hated it.

'Well, it'll be great to see Britt again,' she said ironically. 'It's been a long time.'

'It won't work,' I said. 'It'll never work. We could probably have coped with Dad. I'm pretty sure. He doesn't impose himself. If he can be left in peace with his computer and a cold beer at the table in the garden, he's happy. But Britt. That's a whole different ball game.'

'I wonder what they'll say when they see me here,' Mary-Lou said pensively.

I didn't know what answer to give. I hadn't a clue how they'd react. Would they be surprised? Definitely. But angry? No idea.

I cut some bread and Mary-Lou got out the margarine and cups.

'I wonder too,' I said a few minutes later.

'What?'

'What they'll say.'

'Oh, right.'

I spread the bread and drew yachts on it with the tube of dill caviar. Waited for the water to boil.

'Tomorrow night,' said Mary-Lou, staring out of the window. 'Tomorrow night,' she repeated heavily.

'It's no good, it'll never work,' I said. 'We'll have to do something.'

'Like what?'

'We'll leave. We'll go somewhere else.'

Mary-Lou laughed.

'What do you mean? Will you link up that dreadful motor mower to the wheelchair again? I can't go anywhere, Adam. But we could phone for a taxi and ask them to collect us.'

I took a bite of my bread. And I must have been prompted by my caviar sketch, because without being really conscious of it I said, 'The boat, of course. We can sail away for a few days.'

She gave me a sceptical glance. I recognised that expression and knew I'd given her something to think about.

'Where to?'

'To Fjuk!' I exclaimed. 'We'd have total peace and quiet there. I've always wanted to go.'

That made Mary-Lou really burst out laughing.

'You're not as daft as you look,' she said. 'Fjuk! Nice one, Adam! Yeah, why not? Let's do it!'

She picked up her slice of bread. Saw the caviar boat. Shook her head.

'You'll definitely be an artist, Adam. A con artist.'

What a change of mood that evening! We went from the depths of despair to the heights of elation. The more we talked about Fjuk the better we liked the idea. We started planning. As excitedly as for our first school trip. Mary-Lou wrote a list of what we'd need to take and I strode around the house collecting together all the things I could find: tent, sleeping bags, camping stove, water-proofs, toothbrushes, radio, flower book, drawing stuff, warm sweaters.

'It's too much,' she said. 'We'll have to cross some things off. There won't be enough room in the boat.'

'We probably don't need waterproofs,' I said. 'Nor sweaters, either, I suppose.'

Mary-Lou deleted them.

The food list was huge too. I would have to cycle to the supermarket for it all tomorrow.

'Pity we haven't got any fishing tackle,' I said.

'You could buy some in the shop,' she suggested.

'Add it to the list.'

We carried on till it got dark outside. We seemed to have thought of everything. There was just one small technical problem: we didn't have a mast. We would have to find it.

'We'll sort that out in the morning,' I said.

I had a vague recollection of Dad keeping some gear in the little loft above the outhouse, so I told Mary-Lou I'd climb up and see if the mast was there.

The ladder was hanging at the back. It was enormously long, in two metal sections which you could take apart by pulling out two sprung pegs. Each section made a handy ladder on its own as well.

But for this job I needed the full length. I staggered along balancing the weight and knocking into everything in my path, and eventually managed to get it up the side of the building.

I hesitated for a moment. Climbing ladders was definitely not my scene. But if I avoided looking down I'd probably be all right.

It went okay till I was somewhere near the middle. Then it started to sway. The whole ladder felt as if it was moving. I hadn't reckoned on that. Then it made a sudden lurch and slid along the wall. Came to rest at an angle. I had a hollow feeling in the pit of my stomach. My hands were clutching the sides.

'Just keep still!' Mary-Lou called.

I stood absolutely motionless. I knew I might go crashing to the ground at any second. My legs were shaking. I lowered my head on to the rungs so that my whole body was supported by them. The swaying stopped.

'If you go really gently now it won't move any more.'

I lay motionless a few minutes longer. Then I extended one foot as slowly as I could up to the next rung. It found a hold. The same with the other foot. Sweat was dripping off my brow. I closed my eyes. Carried on crawling up. At last I could touch the solid wall. I felt all over the hatch and was ready to unlock it when I realised I'd forgotten the key. Damn! I banged my fist on the hatch in sheer frustration.

'What's wrong?'

'The key for the padlock! I forgot it.'

'Where is it?'

'In the hall. All the keys are hanging under the fuse box.'

'What does it look like?'

'It's the smallest. There's only one like it.'

'Wait there. I'll go and get it.'

The wheelchair disappeared across the lawn. I closed my eyes again. Tried to think of something pleasant but nothing came to mind. It seemed ages before she returned.

'Is this the one?'

I peered at the key she was brandishing.

'Looks like it.'

'Can you catch it if I throw it up?'

'I'll try.'

She threw it up to me and it came flying past about two feet away. I didn't dare reach out for it. It struck the wall and fell to the ground.

'I'll have another go,' she said, wheeling herself over to pick it up.

'Aim to hit me with it,' I said.

She took aim and threw again. Really hard this time and it came straight at me. It hit me in the ribs and I managed to move one hand and grab it.

'Well done!' she cried.

I put the key in the padlock. It was the right one. The hatch opened and I slithered in and collapsed in a heap on the floor.

'Can you see the mast?'

I gradually recovered myself and looked round the dusty loft. I remembered there was nearly always a wasps' nest up here. I lay where I was and ran my eyes over roof and walls. No sign of any nest.

'Can you see it, Adam?'

I fumbled around on the floor and found something that felt like a round pole. I lifted one end. Sneezed a couple of times. Then called, 'I've got it!'

I started pulling it out and feeding it bit by bit through the hatch.

'Watch out below!' I yelled.

The long mast slid to the ground with a thud, and stayed upright leaning on the wall. The cables that hold it in place slapped against the wall a few times, but soon went quiet.

'Here comes the sprit now,' I shouted and heaved out a smaller pole through the hatch. I heard it land.

'Brilliant,' Mary-Lou shouted.

'Good.'

'Can you get back down the ladder?'

'No.'

'How are you going to get down then?'

'Don't know.'

So, I thought, now I was on my own. I'd never get down from there again.

I had no idea how long I stayed up in the loft. Half an hour, two hours, half a day. I wasn't interested in the time. Time didn't exist. I sat there in a feverish haze, miles away from the murmuring summer day outside the hatch. It was as if I hadn't got any arms or legs. My whole body was as floppy as a jellyfish on the beach. Only people who suffer from vertigo themselves would understand. Mary-Lou's voice penetrated through to me now and again from somewhere far away.

'Adam?'

' … Yes?'

'You have to make an effort.'

' … I can't.'

'You've got to go to the shop. And rig the boat. We've got loads to do. Adam!'

'I can't.'

'But Britt will be here soon.'

Slowly I came to my senses. That name had a remarkable effect on me. The strength flowed back into my bones and I could move my limbs again. Britt! Britt Börjesson! And my dad.

'Britt!' I cried.

'Yes,' said Mary-Lou. 'It's today she's coming.'

'Britt!' I repeated, peering out of the hatch.

'Come on, Adam!'

I looked down at her and felt my stomach lurching again. Her chair was spinning before my eyes. I quickly pulled my head in, like a snail confronted by imminent danger.

'Come out backwards!'

I turned round cautiously inside the loft and reversed out towards the square of light in the wall.

'Britt,' I muttered.

'That's it!'

I could feel my feet groping their way over the top of the ladder.

'Go on! You're nearly there!' she shouted.

I found a tread with one foot. Mary-Lou directed. I moved my other foot. Let it find its way down. And when it hit the next rung I heaved a sigh and took a rest. My legs and bum were out. That was something.

'Good! Carry on exactly like that,' she said.

And so I inched my way down the ladder, at an agonisingly slow pace, with my eyes tight shut. At times my legs were trembling so much that I had to stop. Then I thought, *Britt! Britt!* And could go on a bit further.

When I finally made it to the ground, Mary-Lou clapped. I bowed like a circus artiste. The man with the rubber legs.

'Now we have to get a move on,' I said.

The final thing I did was to leave a note on the kitchen table. I locked the door and left the key in its usual place in the gutter. As we went down to the jetty I could envisage my father's surprise at the wheelchair ramp. And at the lack of door sills. But it wouldn't do him any harm to have something to puzzle over during his long weekend break.

3

There was very little breeze at all, but it was blowing from the south-east so we had it diagonally astern and the boat was making slow progress over the glittering water. It was laden as if for a round-the-world trip. Mary-Lou's wheelchair was lying folded in the bows. I wondered what people would make of us if we met another vessel.

I turned to watch the red cottage and the wooden jetty gradually slipping away from us. I saw Siv and Ruth pottering about in the shade of the trees. Dad and Britt will soon be there to look after you, I thought.

The big spritsail was hanging out at right angles from the boat. The sprit itself was like a boathook, or rather a spear, set diagonally across the top of the sail. The sheet was slack. I knew these sails weren't the best in the world, but they looked good. They suited old boats.

Mary-Lou was reclining in the stern, where Adam's Agency had fitted out a comfortable seat with Britt's hammock cushions.

With the tiller under her left arm, she had a resolute look, the way I imagined a captain should look when embarking on a long voyage.

She gave the sail an appraising glance. Wasn't satisfied with the angle and asked me to haul it in and get the sprit to lie straight in the hoops. She let out the foresail but it didn't help. The boat was only moving sluggishly.

When we got round the point the wind increased slightly, perhaps to about five miles an hour, and shifted to the south. The sail flapped a few times. Mary-Lou pulled it in tighter. I could sense the boat picking up speed, you could feel a gentle shudder through the hull.

The water rippled past the bows. The sun was like a little yellow golf ball that someone had chipped up into the blue sky. It was perfect weather. An ideal day for sailing. Not another craft in sight all the way to the horizon. I closed my eyes and it was like entering a dream-world. I wasn't just on Lake Vättern but also in the Pacific and the Indian Ocean. I felt completely free. I could sail anywhere. To the West Indies, to Australia, to Fjuk. This was how it should always be. If only you could always live like this. Just sailing. No November mornings with Stockholm enveloped in darkness like a damp blanket that would never lift. No more soporific days at school when you wondered what the sense of it all was. No more trying to decide whether to buy pea soup or rice pudding at the ready-meals section in the supermarket just before seven. None of that any more. Just sailing into the sun, just Mary-Lou and Adam. We could easily live like this, sailing from one deserted island to another, going ashore in the sunshine, eating grayling from the clear waters of Lake Vättern.

'This is how it ought to be,' I said, screwing up my eyes to look at Mary-Lou.

'It already is,' she replied.

Her hair was blowing forward, as if it was trying to sail faster. She was wearing a T-shirt and jeans and a blue and yellow lifejacket, the same as me.

'It's good to have some wind.'

'We could do with a bit more. But we're lucky we're not having to tack. These boats really only go when the wind is behind them.'

'I remember you once tacking across the bay in a storm and Dad and me standing on the jetty. Our hearts were in our mouths, but you just laughed and said you liked a gale because it made you feel so alive. I'll never forget that. Nor will my dad.'

'Did I really say that?' she remarked with a smile.

'Yes,' I replied. 'Don't you remember?'

I reached out under the sail and felt in one of the crates. I found a bunch of bananas and broke off two and threw one to Mary-Lou. She laid it down beside her. I peeled mine and ate it.

She indicated ahead over my shoulder and I turned and saw how close we had come to The Maiden. It really did look like a whale basking in the water. From our jetty it seemed so tiny. Like a rock in the water that at most you might just about be able to sit on. Now you could see that there was a whole world out here too. A landscape of grey rocks, white birds and bird droppings. It was the realm of the gulls.

'I don't think we can go ashore here,' I said. 'I have an idea it's a nature reserve.'

'No, we skirt The Maiden and then have a straight run to Fjuk.'

'Right you are, Cap'n.'

As we rounded The Maiden we couldn't hear one another speak for all the screeching birds. I didn't know whether it was because we were disturbing them or whether they were always that loud. The gulls hung over the island like a living parasol, almost motionless and transparent in the sky.

I had a sudden impulse to try and capture them on paper. I hunted out my pad and quickly sketched a whole flock of gulls and then filled in the island. It was more or less the same colour as the pencil.

Mary-Lou put the tiller over and I felt the boat heel and the sail flap a few times before the boat obeyed and picked up speed. The wind felt lighter now that it was coming direct astern but it was actually stronger out here. We were heading due north. The ripple at the bows was more pronounced.

I finished the sketch as The Maiden gradually fell away from us. I held up the pad to Mary-Lou. She looked delighted.

'That's really good, Adam!' she shouted.

I was pleased myself and turned the page to draw her as she sat in the stern with her hair blowing about her face. I checked her through my viewing frame. She stuck out her tongue and laughed at me, and I thought I detected a new quality in her laughter. It wasn't what I'd been hearing this summer, kind of strained and artificial. This was like her old summer laugh, the one she used to have.

I laughed back.

'We should have had a flag,' I said, gesturing towards the stern with my pencil.

'It wouldn't look right on this boat,' she said. 'It's only pleasure craft that fly a Swedish flag.'

'Who said anything about a *Swedish* flag? I mean one of our own, like a pirate flag. You know, a black one with a white skull on it.'

I sketched in a flag. But I put a big black seagull on it instead of a skull and crossbones. It looked really cool fluttering there behind her and when I showed her what I'd drawn she laughed even more.

'We ought to christen the boat too,' she said. 'Or has it got a name already?'

'No, it hasn't.'

I leant over the side and took a handful of water and sprinkled it over the boards.

'I name this ship the *Black Gull*,' I said solemnly.

I had loads of pictures of Fjuk in my mind's eye. All my imaginary childhood boats anchored there. In my dreams I'd been there so often, wandered barefoot along its beaches, watched the red ball of the evening sun dipping into the lake. I'd slept beneath the dense fir trees and woken to the dawn chorus. If there was a real treasure island anywhere on Earth, it was Fjuk.

I could feel the tension mounting inside me as the island loomed larger. Maybe I was afraid it wouldn't come up to my expectations.

We were approaching from due south and initially you'd think it was a single island. Mary-Lou steered along the eastern side and only when we were right up to them did I see the way they sort of glided apart to form three separate islets.

'This is called Jällen,' she said as we passed the first.

It was covered in trees, pine and spruce and aspen. Next came Mellön, which must mean middle island, floating on the water. This was quite different, covered in funny dwarf deciduous trees which I thought might be limes. It looked like an impenetrable mini-jungle.

Then there was a narrow sound separating the last island, Skallen. This was the main island, the biggest, with a white-painted lighthouse rising from the centre. This was where we were headed. This was the hermit's island.

I scrutinised it eagerly as if expecting the old man suddenly to appear on one of the flat rocks.

'How long ago was it when he died?' I asked.

Mary-Lou was concentrating on steering the boat as we approached land. I could see her scanning the water ahead of us.

'Who?'

'The hermit.'

'Thirty years, I think,' she said. 'He was over eighty when he died.'

'Did he really live out here all his life?'

'Yeah, nearly anyway. What was so weird was that he originally came out here to die. A doctor must have told him he only had a short time to live. He was advised to spend as much time in the open air as possible. So he came here to die in peace.'

'But he didn't die?'

'No.'

'Very mysterious,' I agreed.

'Though some people said he came because of an unhappy love affair.'

'Oh, right.'

'You go for'ard and keep a lookout for rocks,' she ordered, in an authoritative voice that left me no choice but to obey.

'Aye, aye, Cap'n!' I replied, crawling over the packages and crouching in the prow. The island was completely surrounded by rocks.

'It's fine,' I called, 'but don't go in any closer.'

The boat was sailing slowly and gently along the shore. The wind had eased off again and the light southerly breeze struggled to fill the heavy spritsail. Mary-Lou rounded the north of the island and luffed into the wind.

'There's our harbour!' she cried.

I could just make out a slight break in the line of the beach, the tiniest gap, and beyond it a calm lagoon of smooth water.

She put the tiller hard over and the boat eased its way into the opening.

'Shall I reef the sail?'

Mary-Lou shook her head.

'There's barely any wind in here at all.'

It was true. The breeze dropped as we entered the bay. The foresail flapped and we soon lost speed. We were right in the eye of the wind. For a minute I thought I would have to row us in the last bit, but then Mary-Lou somehow managed to catch a puff of wind and we gradually approached a long stony beach.

When we were a few metres off I jumped out and hauled the boat ashore. I imagined myself as Adam the Hermit, arriving on the island to live in peace and tranquillity with my handicapped girlfriend.

I carried the wheelchair ashore, and then the sleeping bags, tent, plastic crates of food and all the other paraphernalia. Leaving everything in a heap on the beach, I finally went to get Mary-Lou. I took her on my back and she clung on like an animal, sliding off when we were safely on the beach to stand beside me with her feet sinking into the shingle.

We looked around us, holding on to each other, saying nothing. The little channel between the islands was like a scene out of *Robinson Crusoe*.

The island was bigger than I had envisaged it. Yet not too big. It was encompassable. From one side you could more or less see or guess where the other side was. It was a nice liveable size. I caught a glimpse of what looked like a path that must lead up to the lighthouse.

'Shall we start off by exploring?' I suggested.

Mary-Lou sat in the chair and I pushed her. No roots on this path anyway, with only heather either side.

There was more grass as we neared the lighthouse. I was keen to examine the flora. Small bluebells grew here but none of the big harebells like at the Bronze Age. I saw a plant similar to wild chervil that might have been wild carrot, and here and there some metre-high yellow mulleins, like living lighthouses themselves.

'Look, there's some "last chance",' said Mary-Lou, as we came to a large clump of willowherb as flaming red as a bush fire.

I wheeled her over to them.

'Time's passing,' she said, inspecting the crimson flowers.

More than half the blossom on the stem was fading. So this summer would soon be at an end too. The one that should never end.

We went up to the lighthouse. An enormous iron anchor stood on the hill beside it, with a metal plate that said, *'He withdrew from the trials and tribulations of the world to isolation on Fjuk, where he spent more than fifty years of his life in quiet contentment.'*

Well, I thought, he's got his own statue anyway, an anchor statue.

We looked out across the water. It was a great feeling standing here, on a hilltop in the middle of a vast lake. I wondered if it felt the same if you stood there every day for fifty years. I thought I could distinguish our point. It looked very small and remote, just one green line among all the others on the horizon.

'What does tribulations mean?' I asked.

'Worries, I think,' said Mary-Lou.

We took the same path back through the heather. The island was mostly flat rock but I could see some parts were more fertile. There were superb pine woods.

'They say all the trees were planted by the hermit,'

Mary-Lou said when I drew her attention to them.

We found ourselves a place to pitch our green tent near the beach, behind some wild raspberry bushes.

We were starving. I heated up a sachet of minestrone soup on the camping stove. Mary-Lou was picking raspberries and stuffing them in my mouth. The sun would soon be setting.

'Do you think your dad and Britt will have arrived by now?' she said.

Blowing on the soup, I replied, 'Dad'll be sitting on the jetty swigging a cold beer and Britt will probably have started cleaning out the privy.'

'Did you tie up the boat properly?' Mary-Lou suddenly asked, giving me an anxious look.

I grinned at her.

'This isn't an adventure film, Mary-Lou. If it was, the boat would have been swept out into the lake by now. This is just normal reality. It's the only film you and I will ever be in. Nothing like that can happen here.'

We sat by the shore until the sun was floating on the burning waters of the lake like an orange beach ball. The sky arched over it like a gigantic crimson throat. I imagined Mary-Lou was seeing and feeling the same as I was. That she too was pondering what I couldn't comprehend: that it was just us, Adam and Mary-Lou, in the centre of a whirling universe.

We stayed there till all the air had leaked out of the ball and it had sunk into the depths, and the darkness enveloped us in its silent embrace. And longer, till all we were aware of was the sound of wing-beats, birds or bats, we couldn't be sure. Even longer, till the whole lake finally fell asleep with a sigh and the wavelets drowsily murmured on the warm shingle of the beach. Then, when we could hear our own breath, I kissed Mary-Lou. I was kissing the whole of that cursed wonderful summer. I was surrendering myself and I felt Mary-Lou doing the same. We kissed each other for several minutes, lying on the beach of our very own desert island in the middle of the world. Perhaps even longer.

We were woken by the scorching heat in the tent. There was a fly walking on the outside of the roof. It looked like a black fridge magnet. I hurried to unzip the flap and let in the summer day. My face felt swollen. I'd been dreaming about the hermit, but the dream had dissolved just before I woke up and now it was impossible to recapture. I could feel it sliding away from me. We'd been asleep for ages. Perhaps because we didn't bed down till it was nearly light.

I crawled out of the tent on all fours and sat in the shade of a tree. Mary-Lou emerged a few moments later. We didn't speak. After a while I picked up the saucepan and went through the bushes to the lake to get some water. The *Black Gull* was at rest on the beach. The lake was as smooth as glass. We'd found a superb campsite, only a few steps from the shore and yet so secluded. When I came back I poured some spirit into the stove and managed to spill almost as much again. When I lit it the grass caught fire and I had to douse it with the water. So I had to go and fetch some more.

'Coffee?' I asked as I lowered the pan on to the gently hissing flame.

Mary-Lou nodded.

I took out a sachet of *café au lait* and nipped off the end with my teeth and poured the powder into Mary-Lou's mug. I put an Earl Grey teabag in my own.

While I was waiting for the water to boil I made some sandwiches. The butter had nearly melted and spread itself on the bread unaided.

As I was eating I noticed that my lips felt odd, sort of thicker than normal. Then I remembered why and glanced shyly at Mary-Lou who was sipping her milky coffee.

'Is it okay?'

She nodded.

'It must be a new brand, I think. At least there was some ad for it on TV in the spring. Reduced price.'

'It's fine.'

I picked up my mug and went and sat down next to her. I put my arm round her but she pulled away with a groan.

We went down to the pebbly beach and brushed our teeth. I rinsed my face several times in the clear cold water. It was like a miracle. I could feel my brain cells waking up. My lust for adventure returning.

'What shall we do?'

She could tell from my voice that I had lots of ideas.

'You decide,' she said.

'Let's explore the island, then. And see if we can find any trace of the hermit.'

'I've heard you can see where his house was.'

'Okay. Let's look for that.'

I wheeled her as best I could over the flatter areas above the beach. We were lucky and soon located the foundations of the house. A frame of square stones forming a wall poking up through the grass. And loose stones lying around on the ground. How tiny it must have been, much smaller than one room in a modern house. I remarked on it to Mary-Lou.

'They say he lived in an old wooden kiosk he got in town and brought out here himself. He had a boathouse too. It was made out of lake boats sawn in half and propped up against one another. But I don't imagine there'd be anything of that left by now.'

It made me feel sad to stand contemplating the remains of a whole life. Of fifty years here on the island. But perhaps that's exactly how it should be. You shouldn't leave any personal traces behind. The hermit planted trees, a whole wood rustling out here for years to come.

'Do you think he was happy?' I asked.

She shrugged her shoulders.

'Dunno. Maybe. People say he was really kind. Boats would put in here now and again, of course. He was always friendly to visitors.'

'Do you think he kept chickens?' I suggested excitedly.

She considered it, but shook her head.

'They used to collect gulls' eggs on the islands in the old days.'

'I wonder how it would be to live like this and be on your own all the time, listening to the birds and the waves and the wind in the trees. Always being surrounded by natural sounds. Living on what nature provides. Eating gulls' eggs in the spring.'

'It's a bit different from town life,' she said.

'What do you think he did all day?'

'I think he probably had stacks to do. Much more than many people living on their own in a town. They just sit indoors and look out of the window. He had hundreds of things to take care of. Boats and nets and garden and shovelling snow and cooking meals. And he had to look after the lighthouse too.'

'Was that his job, looking after the lighthouse?'

'Apparently. Though he only got it because he was here, of course. That's what people said. That it wasn't exactly necessary. Not like in the past. In the nineteenth century there used to be several lighthouse families living out here. There'd have been up to twenty people on the island.'

'No way!' I found it hard to believe that this little uninhabited island could have been full of human life a hundred years ago. Twenty people! The island must have been almost overpopulated.

My immediate reaction was that part of the magic of Fjuk was lost because of all those people. Then I realised that it made the island even more fascinating.

'And now there's only you and me living here,' I said.

'And I should think we'll be left in peace,' she replied, looking out over the mirror-like water. 'At least, no boats will be able to get here in these still conditions.'

We went down to the water's edge again in the heat. I didn't know what the air temperature was, which was annoying because I reckoned it must be the hottest day of the summer, probably over thirty degrees. Then I noticed I hadn't got a watch either. So in the end I decided to give up bothering about such details.

Mary-Lou sat in the shade of some alder trees and wrote in her brown notebook. I went and got my pencil case and sat down on the beach to sharpen my pencils. They were in quite a bad state, especially the soft B ones. I was very methodical about it, turning them over and over and paying careful attention to how the points were shaping up.

There was a lot I wanted to sketch on the island. I wanted to document the hermit's life, draw what he must have seen. But considering the various subjects, I realised they might just remain separate individual elements, fragments of a whole. I was somehow too close, inside the frame. I ought to take the boat and row out and sketch the island floating on the water like an ossified ship with the white lighthouse as a funnel and the pine wood as sail.

Meanwhile I decided to try my hand at our boat on the beach. I used a 6B for the first time and the lead seemed almost to flow into the paper. It made fat black lines that suited the character of the boat amazingly well. I worked on it concentratedly for fifteen to twenty minutes, the tarred planking, the mast, the rope running up the beach, the placid lagoon in the background. Then stopped immediately it felt finished. Holding the pad away from me to get an overview, I decided it was one of the best I'd ever done.

'Shall we go in the water?' I proposed, leaning over to Mary-Lou and wiping some beads of sweat off her face.

'I'd love to. I'm sweltering.'

She closed her notebook and put it down.

I wheeled her to the water's edge but as I was about to lift her out she told me to wheel the chair into the lake.

'Then you can practise your swimming,' she added.

I had no desire to swim. Not here on the island. It felt all wrong. Did Robinson Crusoe take swimming lessons? I waded out pushing Mary-Lou's wheelchair in front of me and could feel it was a lovely sandy bottom. So surprising. Where did all these sandy bottoms come from?

'Gosh, it's cold,' she said as the water rose up her legs.

When it got up to the seat she suddenly heaved herself out head first into the water, striking out wildly with her arms. Water sprayed up around her and she splashed it at me. I yelled for all I was worth, tried to escape but it was already too late. She was laughing at me. For a split second it reminded me of another day, another summer, when she'd done exactly the same, splashed water all over me.

I dived in and did some spontaneous fast strokes almost without thinking about it. I think it was arm *and* leg strokes. It came more easily than ever before.

'Adam!' she cried. 'You're swimming!'

I grinned at her. 'A few strokes in a row don't mean you're swimming. I was just pretending.'

But she wouldn't listen to me.

'Do it again! The same again!'

I did as I was told. Braced myself. Launched myself forward. Made some movements with my arms and legs. And on the point of standing up I did a couple more, because I could feel it was actually working.

'Five!' she yelled. 'You did five strokes, Adam!'

'Did I really?' I said, hardly able to believe it. 'Five strokes. Hell. Incredible. How many do you need for a badge?'

'You can swim, Adam. Do it again. A bit slower if you can.'

I was in a dream, counting to five over and over again. I didn't take in what she said at first. Then I gathered myself and had another try. Less of a launch, slightly slower strokes. The water felt warmer now. Mary-Lou was counting out loud.

'...four ...five...six...seven! Go on! Stretch properly! A bit more! Brilliant! Think of Britt Börjesson!'

That's what I did. I did quite a few strokes in her honour. Then I felt myself taking in water and starting to sink. I stood upright in a fluster.

'How many?'

190

'Fourteen.'

'Fourteen?'

'You can swim!'

'Fourteen? You're not having me on, are you?'

'No, honestly. You're swimming really well. Your technique's fine. All you have to do now is practise. And you're an expert at that. The more you practise, the more confident you'll be. I bet you'll be able to swim fifty metres this summer.'

'Fifty metres! You must be joking.'

She looked out over the sound.

'That's about as far as from here to Mellön.'

I surveyed the distance to the wooded island the other side. I realised what had happened. I'd stopped being paralysed by fear. I'd forgotten to think I couldn't swim. I'd simply forgotten to be afraid. It was like learning to ride a bike when you were little. As long as you believed it wouldn't work, you'd keep falling off.

'No,' I said, 'not as far as that. Not to Mellön.'

'Do you feel like helping me with some exercises?'

'You bet,' I replied. 'On the beach?'

'No, in the water. Though a bit further in than this, maybe.'

We moved a little nearer to the shore. I was still shaken by my sudden progress as a swimmer. But pleased that Mary-Lou wanted to exercise. It was the first time she'd actually suggested it herself.

I helped her to sit on the sand with her legs out in front of her. She put her hands flat on each side and started raising herself up and down. She did five lifts and then a pause. Repeated it over and over again. Then she turned on to her stomach and did a long series of press-ups. I stayed close by her, ready to catch her if she lost her balance.

'Aren't you going to do any leg exercises?' I asked as she rested on all fours.

'My arms are more important,' she panted. 'They're what I propel myself with. The wheelchair was really tough to start with. Before I'd done any exercise. I was totally shattered. Most people have no idea what it's like suddenly to have to do everything with the upper part of your body.'

'I'd never thought of it like that.'

'I often train in the pool. Swimming mostly. But only with my arms. That's the most useful.'

'So that's why you're such a good swimming teacher!'

'Probably. I used to go to a special centre in Stockholm for over a year.'

'For the handicapped?'

'Yes. I thought I'd try some cycling movements too, but it's a bit deep here.'

We moved to the shallows and she lay on her back and worked her right leg. She bent and stretched it with me pressing against it to increase the load.

'How's that?'

'Try pushing just a bit harder.'

I pressed her leg in, and she pushed it out again. The sweat was running down her face, into the corner of her mouth.

'That's good,' I said. 'A little more. Then we'll do the other leg.'

We rotated her left and right legs, and then she went over to cycling movements with both, bending and stretching as I tried to apply the requisite pressure. It was a punishing exercise, for me too. She put as much into it as she could. Her legs felt surprisingly strong to me.

I cooked spaghetti and heated up a ready-made pasta sauce with tomatoes, garlic and peppers. We ate in the shade under one of the hermit's trees. I was thinking about his life and the time before him, when it had been almost as densely populated here as a town. Perhaps the island had been bare when he arrived. People might have taken everything there was for building and firewood. That's what they did in those days. They felled the forests because they had to. All this heather seemed to indicate that. Heather takes root where the soil is poor, where nothing else can grow.

I mentioned it to Mary-Lou. She said she didn't know how it used to be.

I wondered what it was he'd been looking for out here. Peace and quiet, perhaps. But there must have been something else as well. Something bigger and more significant. What everyone is seeking, deep inside. He must have found it out here on the rocks of Fjuk. Otherwise he would never have stayed fifty years.

When Mary-Lou was sitting writing that evening I

193

decided to go on with the portrait. I leafed through my sketchpad to find it and sat down on the ground to draw without her noticing. A half-smile played around her lips. I recognised that: her internal laughter. At what she was reading or thinking. It was a sort of Mona Lisa smile.

'Are you drawing me?' she exclaimed when she looked up.

'I'm just finishing it off.'

'Can you do it? I'm not sitting the same at all.'

'It's almost better here, with the boat and this little bay. I haven't started on the background yet.'

'But what about the flowers?'

'It's more natural with your notebook.'

'Do you really think so?'

'Absolutely. It looks like you. I think you ought to have the notebook on your lap. You usually do.'

'I want the flowers as well,' she said stubbornly. 'You can draw them in above the notebook.'

'Okay,' I sighed.

I rubbed out the vague outline of the wine bottle but left the flowers in. I sketched the notebook. I congratulated myself on deciding to work so slowly. I felt that I was at last mature enough to do the difficult part, Mary-Lou's face. Her inquisitive eyes. Her straight nose. I noticed she had a little sore on her lower lip.

I had drawn hundreds of eyes, noses and mouths. I knew how to form them with lines and circles and shadows. That's what made it so difficult: it could easily turn into any nose at all.

I gritted my teeth. Persevered silently and single-mindedly. Then gave my hand a rest and just gazed at her.

'I'd like to create something permanent too,' I said. 'Something that would enrich others, something that would benefit the world. Like the hermit with his trees – well, with his whole life. His way of living was so simple and down-to-earth. He gives us something to think about, even though he's been dead for so long, don't you agree?'

'But you can draw, Adam. You'll be an artist and produce paintings that'll make people understand what matters in life.'

'Do you really think so?'

'Of course,' she said, as if it was the simplest thing in the world. 'You'll paint beautiful sad pictures that'll make people stop and take notice.'

'Why sad?'

'Because life is a sad story. There's a minor key running through the whole of existence. Most people try to ignore the fact. With sweets and crisps and soap operas on TV, the things people comfort themselves with. But you can hear the key, Adam. You're one of the ones who dares to listen. You can paint life. You see what everything's *really* like.'

I had to mull it over before I saw exactly what she meant. A minor key. Sadness, depression. A despondency that rose to the surface when you were least expecting it. The way I felt sometimes when I was at home alone and dusk fell over Stockholm. Like the blues music Dad played on CD. Like some rock songs, the best ones. Like

'Imagine'. I thought I understood. I asked her whether that was the sort of thing she had in mind, the moods conveyed in rock songs, and she nodded.

'Would that make anything better, me painting beautiful sad paintings?'

'Yes, that's how we grow, by hearing music like that, reading books like that, seeing pictures like that. They fill the emptiness around us. It helps us to recognise ourselves in things that are problematical. We have to. Otherwise life is just an empty bag of sweets that in the end explodes in your face so that you have to jump in a taxi to the nearest mental hospital or pop some pills.'

'Not a bad vocation,' I said pensively, to my own astonishment. At last I knew what I wanted to do! I wanted to paint pictures. Create my own pictures and show them to others. What if you could actually make a living doing that!

I sat in silence for ages letting my pencil work on the face while my brain was busy considering what we'd been talking about. It sounded right. It was the sort of thing I wanted to try. Be an artist if I could. I was getting a likeness to her face now, but proceeding very cautiously. I thought the eyes and nose were okay. The mouth had an odd expression, but it would do for the time being. I changed to a softer pencil and started filling in the background. I tried to remember how I'd done the sketch of the boat against the lagoon, so I could rekindle the same feeling I had then. That's what I wanted Mary-Lou's background to be like.

*

196

We went to sleep early but I kept waking up because of the heat in the tent. In the end I crawled out, dragging my sleeping bag behind me like a tail. I laid it beside the tent, fell on top of it and was asleep immediately.

When I woke up the sun was high in the sky. Mary-Lou was sitting a little way off from the tent and smoking a cigarette. She had her black bikini on and her hair was sopping wet.

'Morning, sleepyhead,' she said.

'Have you been awake long?'

'I've been in the lake and done some exercises.'

'I'll make breakfast,' I said and stumbled over to the pan lying under the tree.

I lit the stove, put the water on, made a shrimp-paste sandwich for Mary-Lou.

'I haven't put any butter on it, because it looks so disgusting.'

'It's fine without.'

'I'll take a quick dip.'

I ran down to the lake and when I came back a few minutes later the water had already boiled and Mary-Lou had made the tea and the coffee. She sounded in a very good mood and commended my choice of coffee.

'It's actually very good, Adam. Fancy being able to sit out here on a deserted island drinking *café au lait*.'

'And smoking Marlboro ...'

'I know, it's bloody insane. But that's how it is. I'm going to stop. I've only got three left anyway.'

We didn't say anything for some time, as if we were an old married couple who knew each other's minds.

Then she suddenly said, 'D'you remember when we met in the spring, outside McDonald's?'

'Of course.'

'It probably sounds stupid and you mustn't be offended, Adam, but I couldn't quite place you. Even though you said your name and all that.'

'Maybe it's not surprising when you think of what you'd been through.'

'It wasn't just because of that. I simply didn't remember you. I remembered lots of other friends. I had so many there and you weren't around all that often.'

'Every summer.'

'Yes, but only for a week or two. When your dad was on holiday.'

'Yes, but every summer, Mary-Lou.'

'Do you think I'm stupid for saying that, Adam?'

'No, not stupid, but I do think it's strange. Because you were everything to me. I thought about you nearly all the time. When I was longing to come out to the country it was you I was longing for. And then . . . when you weren't here any more, everything reminded me of you.'

'I had to think for quite a while before I remembered who the Stockholm boy who suffered from vertigo was. I could recall that, the giddiness. Then it came back to me. Where you lived and so on. But not really what you looked like.'

'I could have drawn you in my sleep.'

'It's weird that people can experience things in such different ways,' said Mary-Lou.

'Yes,' I replied.

And so time slowly passed. We lived our island life, quiet days on Fjuk. The heat prevented us doing much. We didn't move around a lot, mostly just sat on the beach. I whistled 'Imagine'. A little refrain stuck in my head, the bit that goes, *'You may say I'm a dreamer, but I'm not the only one...'*

The portrait of Mary-Lou was gradually gaining more definition but the odd expression round the mouth still remained. Our butter had melted away and tiny bright-red ants had taken over the larder I'd built of stones under a tree.

A tick had buried itself in my groin and Mary-Lou wanted to take it off, but I let it stay. I felt it fall off in the tent one night and took it out and dropped it in the raspberry bushes. It was the size of a bumblebee .

There didn't seem to be much animal life on the island. One morning Mary-Lou said she could hear a fieldmouse scrabbling about in the grass outside the tent. But we never saw it. Maybe because the weather was so hot. There was less breeze than a gull's fart, as the saying goes.

It was like being in the Doldrums. I wondered aloud what could have happened to the wind. What if the atmosphere had sprung a leak? The wind might have seeped out of one of those holes in the ozone layer.

She laughed. Winds were being created all the time, she said. It was to do with high and low pressure. The differences between them made the winds blow. The air was sucked from high to low-pressure areas.

Well, it must have been blowing a gale elsewhere,

because there was absolutely no wind here at all. The leaves were hanging straight down from the trees. I noticed the lack of any noise around us. The rustling that's always present without our conscious awareness. The wind caressing the treetops. The slight flutter of a curtain at an open window. The murmur of the waves. All the everyday summer sounds were missing, everything that the wind breathed life into.

'I read a poem about why you can actually hear wind,' I said. 'It's because people who die are changed into grass and trees. It's them making the sound when the wind blows.'

'Do you read poetry?'

'It was in a death notice.'

'You read death notices?'

'It was my grandmother's. She died last year.'

Mary-Lou observed a minute's silence for my grandmother. Then she said, 'Do you believe in such things?'

'I don't know. But all living things are bound together in some way. I mean, you've got to go somewhere when you die.'

'Yes, of course,' she said.

We took pleasure in the stillness, the warmth, the great sense of peace. The water was so smooth that it looked as if you would be able to skate across it to the mainland.

I practised swimming every time I went in. After a few bad days it was beginning to work better again. I set a new record for Fjuk with seventeen strokes and was as proud as Punch.

Mary-Lou and I tried walking up the path towards the lighthouse several times. Just a little way, turning round, trying again. I kept a steady hold round her waist. She walked stiff-legged and with much effort. Took lots of rests. Let me bear her entire weight. But at least she was walking. When she herself wanted to. I accepted that and didn't try to push her any more. But I couldn't help thinking that she would make even greater improvement if she exercised more and I couldn't stop myself pointing it out to her.

'You're walking well,' I said diplomatically. 'We ought to do this every day really. Morning and evening if possible.'

'It's not that important for me, Adam.'

'I mean if you only exercise once a week it's a waste of time. Exercise has to be done more often. The body doesn't take it in otherwise. If you only clean your teeth once a week, they fall out in the end. If you only drink water once a week your body dries out. Don't you see? Your legs don't have time to understand what it is they're supposed to be learning.'

'Shut up, Dr Adam!'

I let the subject drop. I could tell from her voice that she was about to lose her temper with me.

Then we did the craziest thing two people on a deserted island can do: we quarrelled.

It started when I was about to heat the food on the camping stove. Mary-Lou wheeled herself towards the tent and passed so close to the bottle of spirit that she knocked it over. I didn't notice it straight away, only when I smelt it. I grabbed it off the grass but a lot had already run out and there was only a quarter left.

The real reason for us falling out was probably the conversation about exercise. We didn't talk it through to the end properly. Now I was in a bad temper because this carelessness seemed so unnecessary.

Maybe it was also because we were hungry. It could have been much later than we thought. Nearer five than the ten past two we'd guessed at. You should be able to tell from the sun. But now, in the heat of these days on Fjuk, the sun seemed to be high in the sky all day long.

'You might look where you're going,' I blurted out without thinking.

'What the hell d'you mean?' the wheelchair answered with its back to me.

'We might have lost it all.'

'So what?'

'How would we be able to do the cooking?'

'You ought to take better care of your damned bottles!'

'Do you have to drive right through the kitchen?'

'Kitchen? What bloody kitchen?'

Now the chair spun round. Mary-Lou was white in the face.

'Here, where I'm cooking,' I said, gesturing with my arms at the things spread out around me. 'This is a kitchen and you have to look where you're going.'

'Well, I'm sorry I'm so clumsy!'

Then she took a firm grip on her wheels and gave the chair a shove. It hurtled straight through the kitchen.

One wheel sent the pan of mashed potato flying, the other cut our last loaf into two almost equal halves.

'Whoopsadaisy!' she snarled.

'Mary-Lou!' I called out after her.

But there was no point. Not at this juncture. It was our third real row. Civil war was declared on Fjuk.

'Adam! Quick, come and look, a canal boat!'

I ran down to the beach. An old-fashioned white boat was gliding slowly over the water, as majestic as an iron swan. It was the *Diana*. She had turned her engine off so the tourists could enjoy Fjuk. She was less than a hundred metres offshore. It felt very peculiar. As if they were spying on us. A voice over a loudspeaker was talking in English, obviously about the hermit. It carried clearly to where we were: *'He lived here for more than fifty years, all by himself...'*

It struck me as almost unbelievable that American dollar tourists should be hearing this. Was it mere coincidence? I knew the canal boats went past here on their way from the river at Motala to Karlsborg on the other side of the lake, but even so.

What would he have made of it? Would he have deigned to wave to them?

I watched the boat, with its white funnel and Swedish flags. It was quite tall for its narrow width. The tourists filled the two decks the length of the ship. It was easy to see it was built for the Göta Canal, which was no wider than a small river. I wondered how the canal boats coped with the strong winds that often blew up on the lake.

Were the tourists sick over the rail?

Some of the passengers were waving to us. We waved back. That made even more of them wave in response. Then a column of black smoke rose from the funnel and the engines started to throb. It speeded up, people went inside. They had already forgotten us.

As we stood there on the beach watching the *Diana* head west, I felt like a shipwrecked sailor. I really had a sense of distance between us and the people on board that boat. Not just because they were mostly rich Americans. It was a wider gulf than that. Here were Mary-Lou and I, living on Fjuk. We were going to stay here. We were looking for something different. A different meaning to life. We were the hermit's children. *'We are his children!'* I wanted to shout after the boat.

Then it suddenly dawned on me: what if we couldn't get away from here! What if this unusual windless weather just went on and on? It might last for weeks!

I said as much to Mary-Lou, but she didn't think it was anything to worry about. You get blown ashore sometimes when you're sailing, she explained. You just had to lie up and wait till the wind abated. And likewise you could get becalmed. But that would change too.

'But what if it doesn't? What'll we do then?'

'We'll have to swim,' she replied.

Her voice was dripping with sarcasm and pent-up aggression.

The sight of the *Diana* put me in mind of another canal boat that used to ply the lake: the *Per Brahe*. It got caught in a storm one autumn night a long time ago and went to the bottom. I told Mary-Lou about it.

Among the people who drowned that night were John Bauer, his wife Esther and their son Bengt, who was only three years old. It was said afterwards that the boat had been too heavily laden. It had been to Huskvarna to collect a cargo of sewing machines. And at Gränna, where the Bauer family boarded, they loaded barrels of apple pulp.

A few hours later the boat keeled over and sank like a stone with passengers and sewing machines, the lot. No one survived. It lay on the bottom for four years before it was salvaged. It turned John Bauer into a legend. People saw a connection between his tragic death and his remarkable pictures.

Were his drawings melancholy? I wasn't sure. Well, a bit gloomy perhaps. And very ambiguous. You could get completely absorbed by them and spend ages pondering their *real* meaning.

'I remember having one of his pictures on the wall of my room when I was little,' said Mary-Lou. 'A tiny princess riding a giant elk. She was called Tuvull.'

'Tuvstarr,' I corrected her. 'It was Princess Tuvstarr. He did lots of pictures of her. One of them was used as a shampoo ad a while ago. It's the one of her sitting naked by a forest pool and looking at the reflection of her long hair in the jet-black water.'

'I don't think I've seen that one,' she said.

'It would be fantastic to be able to paint like that,' I said.

*

205

I decided to build a handicapped privy out of the driftwood I collected around the shore. The seat itself was a wooden crate that must have been used for fish, and around it I constructed a really smart comfortable frame of poles and branches that you could sit on and support yourself with as you got on and off. The poles were polished smooth by the water and pleasing to the touch. I lashed them fast with bits of rope. It took some time because I had trouble finding enough rope. When it was finished it looked like an old wicker chair.

The privy was in the raspberry bushes, and from it there was a wonderful view over the lake. When Mary-Lou christened it I could hear creaking and cracking. Then the sound of giggling from the bushes.

'What is it?'

'I've really seized up. I think I'm going to die! I held on so tight that I've broken your loo. One of the branches has snapped. Sorry!'

'Doesn't matter,' I said.

More chortling from the raspberry patch.

'Now what?'

'I was thinking about what you said the other day. About the difference between film and reality. If this was a film, scenes like this would be cut. People never go to the loo in a film. Imagine how constipated they must be!'

'I guess so,' I said.

Things were back to normal. No, even better than that. I was beginning to recognise a pattern. After every silly quarrel we seemed to get a bit closer to one another.

As if the sharp words and outbursts of emotion broke down some of the invisible barrier between us.

I don't think I'd ever had such fun as these days on Fjuk. I thought occasionally about the hermit and John Bauer and Mary-Lou. But mostly I didn't think at all. I went around barefoot in my cut-off threadbare jeans hunting for driftwood, sketching, and toying with the idea of making a flag with a black gull on and hoisting it at the highest point of the island. To show that it was ours.

Everything they say about how wonderful it is to live on a deserted island is true. I said this to Mary-Lou but she didn't agree.

'There's no such thing as a deserted island, Adam. This is just Fjuk. Masses of boats and tourists have been here before us. There are no secrets here. There are no undiscovered countries, no new adventures that haven't been experienced before.'

'Life is an adventure,' I replied, 'every day is an adventure. Today is an adventure. Tomorrow will be the beginning of a new one. Our lives are undiscovered countries. Every individual is a continuously developing story.'

I had no idea where I got the words from. I'd never found it particularly easy to express myself. Our time on the island must have turned me into a philosopher.

I didn't want it to end. But I knew it had to. How long had we been here? To judge from our colour it looked as if we'd always lived here. Both of us had acquired an even dark-brown tan. We looked like natives. I remember my father once writing about native islanders somewhere, or indigenous peoples as he called them, and I'd thought it meant they suffered from indigestion.

When we tried to count the days and mornings and evenings they all seemed to merge together. We ran through the things we'd done and the days we'd done them. I tried to recall what we'd eaten. But it didn't help. It was as if time didn't matter any more. As if clocks, hours and minutes had lost all significance. Words like Monday and Sunday and Thursday had no meaning any more. Could that have been how the hermit felt?

'Look! The "last chance" flowers have opened at the top now,' said Mary-Lou.

I could see she was right. The crown had opened up. How were they when we arrived? Hadn't there been two or three rows to go then? Perhaps the hot weather was making the blooms come out faster than usual.

'How long does that mean we've been here?'

'Long enough to mean we'd better sail back home soon,' I replied.

'I don't want to leave,' said Mary-Lou.

We were standing on the path to the lighthouse. I had my arm round her waist.

'Shall we go on a bit?' I suggested. 'You're walking much more easily now. It feels as if you've loosened up.'

'That's only how it seems,' she said.

'No, something's different. You're walking better.'

I was sure of it. Her sunburned skin was stuck to mine. I could feel her body through my arm.

'You're not so tense. You feel more supple all over.'

'Perhaps I've just grown used to you.'

'It's the exercises bearing fruit,' I said.

'Maybe,' she said. 'Maybe not. It varies. Sometimes it's like this, and my body is willing. Sometimes it won't do it at all. I have good days and bad days. This is a good day.'

'But if you go on exercising you'll get over a threshold. That's what all training is about. That's when progress really begins.'

'Not if you've got a spinal injury. The site of the injury determines mobility. That can't be changed. You have a year to find out, the first year. Then you know the score. What works and what doesn't work. We've already talked about that.'

'But in your case it's not definitive. You were lucky too: your injury wasn't total, or whatever the term was that you used.'

'It's called incomplete. The spine was partially damaged, not completely broken. Yes, I was lucky, bloody lucky. But that doesn't actually alter anything very much. I can walk, as you see. I can drag myself along a bit. But it takes a helluva time and a huge effort. It always will. The wheelchair is a lot easier.'

'I don't understand why you won't exercise more. What we've done on the island has obviously worked wonders.'

She looked at me and shook her head.

'Can you walk on your hands, Adam?'

'A few metres. Why, what do you mean?'

'If you did a lot of training, would you be able to walk further?'

'Yeah, of course.'

'So why don't you do it?'

'Why should I?'

'So you can walk on your hands.'

'It's hardly practical.'

'Well, it's hardly practical for me to use my legs. The wheelchair is.'

I didn't say anything. I realised how brainwashed she was by what the doctors and physiotherapists had told her. She went along with it, accepted her role, her wheelchair role. They'd turned her into a package. An apathetic care package. I didn't think it was right. I thought she was giving up. That she was doing so without exploring all her potential. First you have to fight like an animal; after that you can give up.

Won't anyone risk tearing up patients' case notes? Get patients to believe in miracles? Believe in God if they want, as long as it gives them the strength to exercise like the devil. There are no standard people, no standard injuries. No typical patients. Anything is possible. Anything can happen. Both what you want most and what you don't want at all. Miracles are always occurring. People dying of cancer travel somewhere and eat something and are restored to life. The hermit came out here, to a desolate little island, and said to hell with dying. The newspapers are full of stories like that. Life is a film where anything is possible. Why would we go on living otherwise?

I thought all this. But said none of it.

'Can you manage to go on a bit more?' was what I actually said.

'I think we'll stop here and turn back.'

I put on a pan of rice and discovered that I'd bought the type that takes half an hour to cook. I had to fill the burner three times and now there was only a tiny drop left in the bottle. Just enough for the washing-up water – I had a few things with food dried on that needed a good hot soak.

I heated the water while we ate a risotto made with a tin of sweetcorn I'd stirred into the rice. We faced a crisis in the larder. Even the red ants had abandoned us.

'We ought to think about leaving,' I said.

'We can't sail with no wind,' Mary-Lou objected.

'We'll dance a wind dance. This evening, down on the beach. Like the American Indians used to do.'

'You mean a rain dance?'

'No, a wind dance – they had dances for all kinds of weather. For everything, actually. And it nearly always worked. They got what they wanted, because they wished for it so fervently.'

She gave me a mistrustful look. She suspected I was stringing her along, but she couldn't be sure.

'Wouldn't it be better to send a message in a bottle?' she said, holding up the empty spirit bottle.

'Terrific idea!' I exclaimed.

I went and got a pencil and her notebook.

'You can write it.'

'What's the date, do you think? We ought to put that at the top.'

'No idea. Beginning of August.'

Mary-Lou wrote: *Fjuk. Early August.* 'How shall I start?'

'This letter is from the hermit's children,' I dictated.

'Wait, not so fast... All right.'

'... We want to announce a discovery we've made... This island lies exactly in the eye of time... Out here time doesn't exist... Anyone who lives here won't get old...'

'Wait a minute... Okay, go on.'

'You get stronger and cleverer. The sick get well. Unfortunately there's no wind here either, because the eye of time and the eye of the wind correspond...'

'Slow down!'

'Ready?'

'Nearly... Okay.'

'... We don't know whether we'll ever be able to get off the island.'

'Get off the island,' Mary-Lou repeated. 'Right.'

'Whoever finds this bottle is requested to check that we aren't still here on Fjuk.'

We signed our names and took our bottle-mail to the beach. I had torn out the sketch of the boat I'd done and rolled it up and stuffed it in the bottle with the letter. I'd written Adam O. on the drawing. I gave the bottle to Mary-Lou.

'You can throw it out.'

She held on to it for a moment as if it was a baby she was being forced to abandon. Then she raised her arm and threw. It went up in a high arc before landing a little way out in the water with a feeble splash. We stood looking at it. The bottle stayed absolutely still on the placid surface.

'It's no good,' she said. 'Messages in bottles need the wind just as much as sailing boats.'

'I'll see what I can do.'

I waded out to the bottle. Stood behind it and splashed with my hands to make waves. It bobbed up and down and started gradually drifting away.

'It's going!' I cried.

I stayed there quite a while agitating the water to give the bottle a good send-off. Then I rejoined Mary-Lou.

As the sun went down we stood close together on the beach. The bottle was a fair way out but had stopped moving again. Mary-Lou turned towards me, put her cheek against mine, her hands on my hips. I felt her move her feet infinitely slowly, just enough to scrunch on the stones. I followed with tiny, tiny steps. Infinitely slowly she turned herself and me round in the evening sunset. We were dancing a wind dance on the beach.

I woke with a start in the night. I was almost sure it was a noise that had woken me. I think you can tell from the way you wake up. It's more gradual of your own accord, you kind of float up to the surface. This was a jerk. An age-old instinct, the body getting ready to defend itself against an unknown danger.

I sat up in the tent fully alert and listened, but couldn't hear anything. I reached out beside me and felt Mary-Lou's body. Her back was sweaty.

I lay down again. I knew I wouldn't be able to sleep any more. Thoughts began to revolve in my brain. Thoughts I hadn't had for ages. How were Siv and Ruth? Were they still at liberty? Had my father and Britt returned to the city yet? They must have, surely. Was Dad worried about where I was and why he hadn't heard from me? When was the first day of term?

I could feel the spell beginning to wear off. The Fjuk dream was coming to an end.

'What's up, Adam?' Mary-Lou suddenly whispered. She sounded as velvety soft as the night itself, but I could tell from her voice that she was as wide awake as I was.

'Aren't you asleep?'

'No.'

'I thought I heard something,' I said.

'It's the wind,' she replied.

Then at last I heard what it was that had woken me: a gentle breeze outside. Wind in the trees, brushing the grass outside, stroking the wild raspberry canes. And I could hear that the waves had woken up too – there was a soft hiss from the shingle.

The wind was back!

It was a sad morning. Our campsite looked like a rubbish tip. Clothes and sleeping bags all over the place. The tent was flat on the ground, like a punctured air balloon. We were eating as we moved around, each of us with a crumbling sandwich of tinned mackerel in tomato sauce that I'd dug out from the depths of the larder.

We were packing with no great enthusiasm, not thinking about what we were doing. I had to roll up my sleeping bag three times before it would fit in its sleeve. Our minds were on other things. The time that was over. When I began carrying our stuff down to the boat it looked as if we had twice as much as when we came. I stowed most of it in the prow, poking bags down between the bigger things.

'The bottle's gone anyway,' I said, peering out across the lake.

The waves were getting up. The wind was only light but I knew it had changed everything.

I unfurled the spritsail and partially hoisted it, taking hold of the upper corner and feeding in one end of the sprit. I stuck the other in the lower corner at the mast. At least it would be fun to be sailing again, I thought, recalling our magical voyage out. We'll make it to the mainland in this wind in a few hours. I hoisted the little foresail too and let the boat lie there with the sails up. They flapped gently. Mary-Lou was sitting on the beach.

'Shall we go up to the lighthouse?' she said.

'Okay.'

I pushed the wheelchair where we had walked so many times. There's something special about islands. You get attached to them. They're more alive than the mainland in a way. Especially this one, where you could sense the spirit of the hermit.

We stood by the anchor and took our silent farewell of Fjuk. Up here I could feel the wind strengthening. It was even gusting in the treetops of the pine wood.

'We'd better get going,' said Mary-Lou.

She steered the *Black Gull* elegantly out of the lagoon. We passed south of Skallen and Mellön. The sail was full and the foresail was billowing out as if it wanted to make landfall ahead of us. Mary-Lou pulled in the sheet and made it fast to the cleat on the gunwale. When we were clear of the Fjuk islands she put the helm over and set course for the mainland.

The waves were quite big. The wind was blowing astern. You could see it was strong, even though you could hardly feel it at all. We were racing with it, and the boat was rising and falling as the waves overtook us with a swoosh. I glanced at Mary-Lou. She looked blissfully content.

'If we're lucky we'll be running before the wind all the way,' she said.

I tightened my lifejacket round my chest. Then lowered myself on to the sleeping bags and made myself comfortable. I'd intended to do some drawing but my stomach felt queasy as the boat surfed over the waves. I was afraid I'd be seasick if I tried it. I propped myself upright with the tent at my back and watched Mary-Lou. Her face wore a look of concentration, there was a smile on her lips. She had that expression again. The real Mary-Lou, her soul exposed and shining out of her eyes.

She grinned at me when she realised I was watching her. I thought over what I'd learnt about drawing this summer. It wasn't just about making a likeness. Well, it was to begin with, but then you had to add something to the picture. Something you knew about the subject, something you wanted to express. For it to be art.

I looked out across the lake. The contours of the land were like soft pencil lines all around us, like a 3B. We were nearly halfway across now. I turned to see if I was right and saw that Fjuk was already far behind us, like a ghost ship heading in the opposite direction. Beyond the island I could see something that hadn't been there before: a broad dark brushstroke had appeared on the horizon. The sky behind Fjuk was absolutely black. A storm. Even lightning perhaps. I pointed.

'That doesn't look too good.'

Mary-Lou glanced briefly over her shoulder.

'It isn't coming this way,' she said calmly, and relaxed into her seat again. I could tell she was enjoying the sailing. She was in her element now she'd got the old boat up to speed.

But I couldn't take my eyes off the clouds. I focused on the lowering horizon like a police dog. I was thinking how dangerous it would be out on the lake if there was lightning. It always went for an object higher than its surroundings. Nothing stood out more than a lone boat on a lake.

Britt was the most nervous person I knew as far as lightning was concerned. Whenever there was the slightest rumble of thunder she would rush out of the cottage with a pile of magazines and sit in her white Mazda. She would sometimes fall asleep in the car and we would leave her there and shake her awake the next morning. Then she would be livid that we hadn't woken her before.

I don't know how much time elapsed, but after a while the blackness seemed to be spreading across the sky.

'I think it's coming this way after all,' I said.

As Mary-Lou swung round to look, a sudden gust made the boat lurch and she fell against the gunwale, giving her arm a real bash.

'Bugger,' she said.

She slackened the sheet and I thought the boat seemed to move more smoothly. I lay on my stomach and stowed our gear better. Pushed in a few loose clothes. Then turned my attention back to the horizon. I was right about the storm. No doubt any longer. The leaden clouds were blowing across the sky like smoke from a fire. The light over the lake was gradually being dimmed. There was an eerie atmosphere, like night in the middle of the day. The boat was heeling over further and the wind seemed to have shifted. It was now more abeam than abaft. The wheelchair slammed against the boards in the prow.

'It's blowing up,' said Mary-Lou.

She let out the sheet but there wasn't much she could do. I was having trouble simply staying where I was. My body kept slipping sideways.

'Reef the sail!' she called.

I got up on my knees and rolled the lower end of the sail into a sausage and lashed it together. So half the sail was reefed but I couldn't tell whether it was having much effect on our speed. Maybe we should take it down altogether. I was about to suggest this to Mary-Lou when a flash of lightning illuminated the lake. It lasted several seconds. We held our breath. Then came the thunderclap, a heavy prolonged echo resonating from one side of the lake to the other, crashing into the steep cliff at Omberg and fading away with an angry growl.

The wind was still rising. The waves were pounding at the gunwales and the water cascading into the boat. My jeans were soaked through and I was thinking I'd better stash my sketchpad further down, but as I bent over, fumbling among the packages, I started feeling really sick. A strong wave thumped against the boat and knocked me off balance. Thank God I hit the mast, otherwise I'd probably have gone overboard.

'Hang on!' Mary-Lou yelled.

I didn't answer but crawled back to my place, keeping a firm grip on the thwart.

It made me think of an evening when I was little and went out with my dad to lay the net beyond the point. Just as he was lowering it into the water while I was sitting at the oars we saw a similar black storm cloud suddenly gathering on the horizon. Dad rowed for all he was worth. By the time we got to shore we could hardly tie up. The waves were just flinging the boat against the jetty. I remember he was a bit ashamed afterwards because he'd shown his fear. He tried to joke about it. But I could see through him. He hadn't been afraid for himself, but for me.

Another streak of lightning lit up the sky, bathing us in an unnatural white light. I could see Mary-Lou, the boat, Fjuk, the whole lake, fields and houses and roads way up on the mainland. The world was a pale copy of itself. The thunder rolled right over us, heavy and threatening.

I could feel I was frightened. But I knew it wouldn't do to give way to panic. Everything depended on me now. On me and Mary-Lou.

'Can you manage to lower the sail?' she yelled.

'I'll try.'

I hooked my left arm round the mast for support while I hauled in the sail with the other hand. I couldn't ease the sprit out of its hoops but let the whole lot drop down into the boat, pulling it together as best I could.

'Well done!' Mary-Lou shouted.

'What are we going to do?'

'We'll get home on the foresail.'

The lake was rough and unpredictable. It felt as if we were sailing through a forest, through John Bauer's old tree stumps. The boat was no longer going so fast, but not so steadily either. We were being tossed about unmercifully.

I could feel the sickness rising from my stomach. I couldn't do anything, not think, not focus, not apologise. I vomited right in my own lap. Twice. I put my head in my hands. Waited for this internal storm to blow over. I smelt of mackerel and tomato sauce. I was sick again. Then it settled down.

'Feeling better now?'

I nodded and rinsed my mouth with water.

'Your face is grey,' said Mary-Lou. 'Are you scared?'

I shook my head.

'Not really,' I replied.

I didn't say what I was thinking: that I wasn't scared as long as she was sitting there. That it was her handling of the boat that kept me from panicking. I could see that she was in control. Her grip was assured. This was just a different type of weather from what we had before and she was adapting the sailing to the circumstances. As if she were the one deciding, and not the wind. If I were the wind, I thought, I'd be really peeved by a sailor like that.

Yet another flash of lightning and I counted silently to see how far off the storm was. You count five for every mile. It's an old method of reckoning that Britt introduced me to. And I got to five just as my thoughts were drowned out by the peal of thunder. About a mile, then.

'It's going south of us,' said Mary-Lou.

'You think so?'

She had no chance to reply. The boat was suddenly thrust forward and there was a crack, loud and menacing. Something on board had broken. Hell, I thought, we're going to sink! The foresail flew loose. It was blowing straight out from the boat.

'The cleat has snapped off,' she shouted.

I stared at the gunwale on the port side. The little wooden bracket that you wound the sheet round was gone. Just two empty screw holes.

The boat was heeling hard. We were rolling from side to side. The wind was showing us who was in charge now all right.

'We've got to get hold of the foresail,' Mary-Lou yelled.

I looked at the sail flapping to and fro in the wind. She put the tiller over to head up into the wind but the boat wouldn't respond. Without a sail we had no control.

'Come on, Adam, try!'

'Okay,' I said. I crawled on all fours across our gear and when I got into the prow I lay on my stomach and watched the sail whipping back and forth in the wind. I would never be able to reach it.

'Try and grab the sheet!'

I kept my eyes on the white rope and saw that whenever the boat shuddered under the impact of a big wave the rope snaked in across the deck. I would have to make a lunge for it at just the right moment. I crawled forward as far as I dared and leant out over the bows.

Mustn't fall in, I thought, mustn't fall in. Not for anything in the world. How long would you last in these waters, even in a lifejacket? Would you have any chance at all when the waves were surging over you like stampeding bulls?

If only I'd had my father's mobile phone with me. I could have made a call to the lifeboat and told them our foresail was in tatters and the spritsail was furled and asked them to send a helicopter out to pick us up. Though maybe someone had already seen us through binoculars and raised the alarm. I hoped so. Oh, how fervently I hoped so.

The top part of my body was swaying dangerously as I leant out over the bows groping for the sheet. I was nearly retching again, but tried not to think about it. I swallowed. Spat out saliva. Swallowed again. It subsided. I was watching the waves and starting to see a pattern. Big waves made the foresail lose wind. I waited for the right one. A white flash lit up the lake. In the stark glare I could see an enormous dark-green wave bearing down on us. I got set. It broke over us and struck the planking with a thud. The boat hung momentarily in a no-man's-land before hurtling down the crest of the wave. The sail dropped, the rope flicked towards me.

'Now!' screamed Mary-Lou.

I flung out my arm for it.

'Got it!' I screeched.

Then came the thunderclap. A dull boom followed by a drawn-out rumble.

'Don't drop it, Adam. Hang on to it!'

I thought even she was beginning to sound frightened now. I could well understand it. She couldn't do much without a sail.

But when I came crawling back with the sheet clutched in my hand I saw her laughing.

'Well done,' she said.

She took the rope from me and made it fast to the cleat on the starboard side. There was a worrying creak when it took the strain and my first thought was that this cleat would snap off too. Maybe the whole boat was old and half rotten. But nothing happened. The foresail filled out. The boat righted itself. We were sailing again. Admittedly with a loosely sheeted foresail, but we weren't drifting helplessly any more. We had some control over our fate.

'Let's hope it holds,' I said.

'I'll try to make for the northern point instead. We might be able to get into the lee of it.'

I felt as if I was going to be sick again. I could see she was changing course, and that the boat was responding. Into the wind a little, so that it hit us obliquely. The boat heeled right over. I didn't like it. I was about to say so to Mary-Lou when there was another sharp crack.

It was exactly the same ominous sound as before and I just caught a glimpse of the starboard cleat flying away from the boat and being swallowed up by the dark waves.

I was sick a couple more times but hardly anything came up even though my stomach felt as if it was being turned inside out. As through a mist I could see the shape of Mary-Lou rising and falling in time with the waves. She had all her work cut out just to stay in the boat.

'If you can grab the sheet again we can tie it round the thwart,' she cried.

'Aye, aye, Cap'n,' I replied. What else could I say?

It was harder to go forward now. It was like sitting on a wild animal that was trying to throw you off. When I was nearly there we took a vicious blow and I smashed my arm against the wheelchair as I fell.

The foresail was flapping in the wind, the sheet alternately trailing in the water and jerking up in the air. I only had to do what I'd done before, but I knew I couldn't. The almost superhuman strength I'd managed to muster then had drained away. Everything was draining away now. I could feel my face getting hot. Maybe I was feverish.

'I can't!' I yelled.

'Pull the sail itself!'

I held on to the forestay with one hand and tried to seize the sail with the other. I got a grip on the far edge of it but it was flapping like mad. All I could do was hang on to it, nothing else. Least of all pull it in. A flash of lightning blinded me and I waited for the clap of thunder and let it finish reverberating before yelling, 'I can't do it!'

'You must, Adam!'

I lay stretched flat out along the prow. I felt so ill. I could sense myself becoming indifferent to everything. I couldn't really be bothered. It didn't seem to have anything to do with me any more. It could have been happening to somebody else. We were going to die. I wondered how it felt. Perhaps dying was nice. Perhaps it was much better to die than to be pitched about like this. I suddenly wanted to be a tree.

The boat was riding up and over the crests of the waves. I could hear water slopping about in the boat somewhere. Was it leaking? Or was it the waves swamping us? I could feel the boat changing course, but I didn't know whether it was the wind or Mary-Lou getting a response from the rudder. Things weren't making sense any more.

'Adam, here comes the sheet!'

I looked up and saw the white rope flying through the air above me. At first I couldn't see what it had to do with me, but when it flicked up and shot over again I put out my hand anyway and managed to grab it without knowing how.

'Hold on to it!'

I had the rope in my left hand. I couldn't understand why she was making so much fuss, but I swapped hands and crawled back amidships.

'Try to tie it somewhere. Anywhere.'

I looked around. Here was the mast. The good old mast. I was so glad to see it and wound the rope a few turns around it, pleased to be rid of it.

'No, Adam, don't let go! You've got to tie it up!'

I felt I'd had enough now. Just to shut her up I made what I thought might be a clove-hitch and then lay down on the wet sleeping bags. It was so wonderful to lie down. It made me feel warm. I pulled a corner of the spritsail over me and wished Mary-Lou would come and lie down with me as well.

She had a resolute expression on her face. She was struggling with the tiller. Then she dipped down out of my line of vision. It wasn't my problem, I thought, and closed my eyes.

'The thunderstorm's going away,' she shouted.

I didn't really know what she was talking about. She'd have to sail by herself for a while. I had to have a rest.

I'd no idea whether I fell asleep or whether I'd just closed my eyes for a minute. But when I next looked up, everything had altered. The lake was less rough, the boat was moving more slowly, Mary-Lou was keeping a straight course. I could see land behind her, and some big rocks I thought I recognised.

'We've rounded the north point,' she said.

I raised my head and craned forward. Saw our point on the other side of the bay. There were the cottage and the jetty. We were nearly home!

'Bloody hell,' I said emphatically. 'I thought we were going to die.'

Mary-Lou's eyes were on me.

'How are you?'

'A bit better now.'

'It was lucky you caught the sheet.'

'What a gale!' I said.

Mary-Lou laughed.

'No, Adam, a real gale is very different from that. But I agree it blew pretty hard, and there were some strong gusts when the thunderstorm was on top of us. But a real gale would have blown us clean out of the water. I suppose this could almost have been a moderate gale, thirty miles an hour in the gusts.'

'Well, it was damned good luck it wasn't a real gale, then,' I said. 'The boat would never have survived it.'

I sat up and tried to regain control of my body. Everything was drenched. There was quite a depth of water in the bottom of the boat.

I stared again at our point. I could see someone had come out on to the jetty. Someone in a mauve jumper, arms waving.

'Who's that?' asked Mary-Lou.

'That,' I replied, 'must be Britt Börjesson.'

4

I'm not sure how to describe our homecoming. There were so many emotions involved. There was so much all at once. As far as I was concerned, my main feeling was relief at climbing on to dry land again. My father helped me on to the jetty. My legs were the problem. They wouldn't bear my weight. Dad had to hold me up to prevent me collapsing. He hugged me and said how mighty glad he was to see me again. I said it was good to see him too.

Mary-Lou was helped out of the boat by Britt Börjesson. She was as strong as an ox, took Mary-Lou under the arms and hardly flexing a muscle lifted her straight out. Then she leant over the boat again and hoisted up the wheelchair with a slight swing of her body – the way a harbour crane might unload a ship in dock.

'Are you all right?' Britt asked.

'Perfectly, thank you,' Mary-Lou replied, though she turned to Dad and me as she said it.

There was a lot of talk about how worried they'd been. Britt did most of it. In fact she never stopped wittering on. But we were used to that. She said they'd been on the jetty for days keeping a lookout for the boat. And they'd had the radio on all the time. Though I didn't really get that. Did she really think we'd be on the radio?

'We presumed you'd put into harbour somewhere,' Dad explained. 'There's been no wind for days. But you should have phoned.'

'We've been on Fjuk,' Mary-Lou said.

'What day is it today?' I asked.

'Thursday. You've been away nearly a whole week.'

'Oh,' I said.

I thought we'd been away a year. That's how long it seemed. It certainly felt like it as we stood there on the jetty like a couple returning from America.

'Your mother's been in touch,' Dad said to Mary-Lou. 'I told her everything was fine. I didn't want to upset her unnecessarily.'

'Thanks – that was thoughtful of you,' said Mary-Lou.

So it went on. There were lots of questions and lots of answers, all the conventional exchanges for the circumstances. Then when they started running out, when everything had been said that could be said, when we had told our basic story and they had expressed their concern, that's when the real homecoming began.

When we could no longer hide behind the usual pleasantries we fell silent. We were passing the stuff from the boat to the jetty and our words were drying up as the boat was emptying. In the end we felt as if we were standing there naked, as if we finally saw who we were. And we must all have been thinking the same thing: how on earth can we keep this up?

Britt carried on smiling at us. She was beaming in the way that only she could. She screwed up the whole of her face, like a rubber mask. Her eyes disappeared in a smudge of mascara, her lips stretched out like a rubber band. It was easy to believe it was the warmest smile in the world. But if you saw it all the time, as I did, you realised it was only a grimace. To me she just looked like a cat in need of a crap. She only had two expressions of emotion: that hoarse guffaw I hated, and this crapping cat look.

Luckily it occurred to her that we must be starving so she went off to the kitchen.

Dad came more into his own when she'd gone. He asked us how it had been out there on Fjuk and listened properly to our answers. I could see him picturing to himself everything we'd done.

'You ought to write about the hermit,' I said. 'His life-story would really be worth telling.'

'I had actually wondered about it.'

Mary-Lou didn't contribute much. She sat listening and only answered when Dad put a question directly to her. I wondered whether it was because of Britt. It must have shaken her to see Britt again. Then Dad asked her if she'd like to rest for a while before we ate and she nodded gratefully.

'Yes, I would,' she said.

It wasn't till then that I fully appreciated how completely done in she must be after the voyage.

Britt had made a fry-up of eggs and bacon and potatoes, but even though I really liked it I could hardly get anything down. My stomach wasn't on dry land yet. I just picked at the food. And drank vast quantities of water. I felt as if I was pouring half of Lake Vättern into me.

'You must be completely dehydrated,' my father remarked.

'I was horribly sick,' I admitted.

Mary-Lou was dead to the world. She was lying in her bed like a mummy. Not even Britt could wake her.

'Leave her,' Dad said. 'She needs a good rest.'

She didn't wake up until dusk. We heard her moving and I went in to her.

'Hi,' I said, because it felt as if we hadn't seen one another for ages.

She murmured something and curled up into a ball under the blankets. She looked as if she was going to go back to sleep.

'You've been asleep all day,' I said.

She half-opened her eyes.

'Have I? It feels like scarcely any time at all.'

I went on talking to her so that she wouldn't get a chance to drop off again, and gradually I saw her eyes clearing.

'God, I'm famished!' she suddenly exclaimed.

Dad and Britt were sitting at the table in the window. He was reading and she was playing a card game I think was called General's Patience. The whole table was covered in cards.

'Is there any grub left for Mary-Lou?' I asked. 'Though not bacon. She doesn't eat meat.'

'I can make a vegetarian hash,' said Britt, getting up. 'We've got some mushrooms in the larder.'

'There are hardly any mushrooms this year,' Dad lamented. 'Only in the very dampest spots. We found some in the birch bog. They say this heat-wave is the worst since the summer of 1959.'

'There's rain forecast for the weekend,' Britt interjected.

'That remains to be seen,' said my father.

Mary-Lou had chanterelle mushrooms and diced potatoes and onions, and after gobbling up the whole lot went on to make herself three pieces of crispbread with cheese and tucked into them too.

'You must have been ravenous,' said Britt. 'There's an apple cake too. Would you like a piece for dessert?'

It turned out that everyone wanted some. So we were soon all sitting at table enjoying apple cake and hot custard.

'The apples are Yellow Transparents,' said my father.

'That's the tree below the privy,' I explained to Mary-Lou.

'It's been a good crop this year, anyway,' said Britt.

That's how the conversation went on. As if we were one big happy family. We made small talk, as they say. About mushrooms and apples. The window was open and the sounds of the summer evening blended into our chatter. Until Britt took it upon herself to close it, saying there was nothing worse than mosquitoes and they were around, despite the heat-wave.

'And bees,' she added. 'I've never seen so many bees as this summer.'

At ten my father switched on the news. The world

233

was just the same. A plane on its way to Cyprus had to turn back because they had forgotten the trolley of duty-free. The Pope was on a visit to Africa. The water shortage threatened this year's crayfish catch. Two Spaniards were in joint lead in the Tour de France.

'There's a news drought,' my father said.

By half past ten I was dozing off at the table. Dad got up and said he was going to fetch the beds. There were only two bedrooms in the cottage, of course, his and Britt's. With just Mary-Lou and me there it was perfect, but now it was a problem. There were twice as many of us. We couldn't be paired up any old how. I'd thought of that and had assumed Mary-Lou and I could camp in the garden. But I knew I had no desire to go out in the dark and erect a tent.

'I'll give you a hand,' I said.

We walked over to the outhouse. The grass was wet and I said I didn't see how it could be in this dry spell. Even the thunderstorm hadn't brought any rain. Dad started explaining about the air always containing moisture but it not being released until the air cooled. But I still couldn't follow it.

We switched on the light and found the two folding tubular steel beds behind a wall of paint pots.

'You and Mary-Lou can sleep in my room, and I'll sleep in with Britt,' Dad said as we carried the beds between us.

'Thanks, Dad.'

I wheeled Mary-Lou up to the privy. I was almost

asleep as I stood waiting for her. When we came back Dad and Britt had already been down and brushed their teeth. They said goodnight. As he was closing the door of Britt's room Dad pointed with his foot at the strip of paler wood in the doorway.

'I've never understood the need for door sills,' he said.

'They're in the outhouse,' I replied.

Mary-Lou and I made up our beds. There were spiders' webs and dead leaves on them but we ignored that and just climbed in.

'I'm wide awake now,' she complained.

I'm not sure I even answered. I could feel the bed rocking up and down, up and down. Then I fell asleep.

Next morning I saw everything in sharper focus. I slept late and when I eventually staggered out to pee in the willowherb Britt was already slogging away at something and the air resounded to hammer blows.

I sat down on the bench by the cottage to wake up. I saw all the old familiar things with new eyes. The garden seemed a bit alien, as if I'd been away for years.

'Twenty to twelve,' Dad said. 'You've been asleep for thirteen hours.'

He was sitting at the garden table, writing on his laptop.

'I was dead tired,' I laughed.

'Is Mary-Lou awake?'

'Yes, she is,' she said, appearing in the doorway. 'Though she hardly slept a wink.'

235

The ramp was leaning against the end of the house. I went and fetched it and put it back in place. The nails were still in the old door so I picked up one of my dad's wooden clogs and hammered them in to hold it firm. I wondered how it was going to be now, which would have priority, their lives or ours.

When we came back from the privy Britt was by the house. She looked at the ramp with disapproval and then hobbled up it.

'This is damned awkward for anyone who isn't handicapped,' she exclaimed.

I was familiar enough with Britt to know she didn't mean anything special by that. Just a simple statement of fact. That she found it difficult to walk up the board. Probably because she always had slippery loafers on.

But I could feel Mary-Lou physically wince. Her shoulders shot up and her muscles tautened. She was breathing heavily. But she didn't say anything.

When Britt had gone in we went down to the jetty. The wind had slackened and the lake was calm with just a summery ruffle on the surface. The boat lay quietly at its mooring. The only evidence of what it had been through were the marks of the ripped-out cleats on the gunwale. We brushed our teeth and washed.

I fixed us some breakfast, which was a bit awkward because Britt and Dad wanted their lunch at the same time. As soon as my water boiled Britt jumped in and moved my pan to lay claim to the hotplate. Mary-Lou and I took our cups and sandwiches and went and sat outside. We ate in silence. But I was virtually certain we were thinking the same thing: this wouldn't work. It was them or us.

My dad had always had a unique ability to avoid friction or argument. I'd never really understood how he did it until now. He sort of stepped back from the front line and then acted first for one side and then the other. Like a mediator, more or less, agreeing with each in turn. He would maintain a calm and objective outward appearance, but now I realised he was also ingratiating, certainly charming, but even somewhat hypocritical. I thought it was cowardly. But then it occurred to me that I was probably the same. Why is it so difficult to see yourself?

I had a feeling Dad would soon need all his diplomatic skills. There was definitely something in the air. Our dear old garden with its gnarled fruit trees seemed suddenly as fragile as glass. You had to tread carefully: it only needed a few unguarded words, one more obtuse remark from Britt, for everything to explode.

Dad must have noticed it too because he was busy mediating. He was chatting to Mary-Lou very well-meaningly, about her school in Stockholm, about going there as a handicapped person, and Mary-Lou was telling him about the centre for the handicapped she'd been attending. Dad thought the newspapers ought to do an article on it and she agreed. They then went on to talk about the possibility of a series of reports shadowing a handicapped boy or girl. And Dad was wise enough not even to hint that he might be able to write about Mary-Lou.

The next minute he was with Britt, following behind her with the tar bucket as she crawled along the outhouse painting the stone foundation wall. That was the sort of thing that made me feel he went too far.

It didn't help, either. Arguably quite the reverse. The tension in the garden was so palpable that Dad's flitting to and fro simply emphasised it.

It only needed one spark to ignite it.

It was Siv and Ruth who finally caused the explosion.

They were locked up in the chicken run again, of course. I wasn't surprised, in fact I hardly even noticed it because that was how it always used to be. I knew it must have been Britt: she wouldn't want chickens running around her feet.

But Mary-Lou wouldn't have known. When she wheeled herself into the chicken run and looked under the Volvo she called out to me, 'It's completely full of eggs again!'

I fetched a basket from the house and went over to her. I got down on the ground and wriggled under the car and rolled the eggs out to her one by one.

'Eleven!' she cried.

Britt had heard all this where she was painting her black wall. She started hooting with laughter and I could hear her coming over. She went into the enclosure, put her half-full can of tar on the ground and knelt beside it to look under the car. I met her eyes.

'What stupid hens,' she said. 'Fancy hiding the eggs under the car!'

'It was Mary-Lou who discovered it,' I muttered.

I crawled back out. Dusted off sand and feathers. Then picked up the basket that Mary-Lou had filled with eggs and started walking up to the cottage. I took it for granted that Mary-Lou and Britt would be following me. But that was where it all went wrong. They were still in the chicken run. I only realised when I heard Mary-Lou's voice, cutting through the air like a knife.

'It's no more stupid than the people who lock them up in prisons like this!'

'What's that supposed to mean?' Britt retorted sharply.

'What I said. I think people who lock up chickens are stupid.'

'It was me that locked them in,' Britt said icily. 'That's where they should be.'

'But there's any amount of space in the garden. Chickens like being able to roam free.'

'But I don't like it and it's my house.'

'It's Adam's father's house.'

'No, it's mine and his. We own half each, in case you didn't know.'

'So you think you can do exactly as you like just because you own part of his house?'

'Well, as a matter of fact, they're my hens as well. I was the one who bought them and I'm the one who looks after them.'

'I can see that!'

'What do you mean?' Britt yelled. She raised the thick

239

brush dripping with tar. I saw some splash on Mary-Lou's lap.

'What the bloody hell are doing, you old cow!' Mary-Lou screamed.

She kicked out with her left foot, missing Britt's leg but hitting the tall can fair and square. It made a hollow clang as it tipped over. The sticky tar flowed out across the chicken run.

'Bloody girl!' screeched Britt.

'Pack it in!' I shouted.

But I might as well have saved my breath. They neither saw nor heard me. I was afraid something dreadful might happen. Even a fight. Without really being conscious of what I was doing I took an egg out of the basket and weighed it in my right hand.

'Stop it!' I cried. Then I threw it.

I'm not sure exactly what I aimed at, but the egg smacked into the side of the Volvo and the contents spattered everywhere. Mary-Lou and Britt didn't even notice.

Britt bent down to pick up the can. Her hands were black with tar. She grasped one of the arms of the wheelchair and gave it a violent shake. Mary-Lou was rattled backwards and forwards and almost flew out of the chair as she fought to push Britt away.

'You fucking bitch. Let go!'

But Britt had no intention of letting go. So Mary-Lou leant over and bit her on the hand.

'Aaargh!' roared Britt, jerking her hand back.

I picked up another egg. This time I aimed properly.

It hit its target and smashed into Britt's red hair, its yellow liquid trickling down the back of her head and neck.

She swung round in disbelief and stared at me. I was already poised to throw another.

'Pack it in, Britt!' I yelled. 'That's enough!'

I wondered where the devil my father could be. It was high time for the great diplomat to enter the arena. Then I saw him emerging from the privy. He'd been sitting on his backside in there! Here he came with yesterday's newspaper under his arm shambling down to see what was going on. Nice one, Dad, I thought to myself.

I knew he must have heard every word from inside the hut, yet out he came like a blue-eyed innocent, ready to help everyone, to offer comfort and dress wounds. All that was missing was the white flag with the red cross on.

But I clued him in, for the sake of appearances. So then he went dashing into the chicken run and bewailed the sticky tar on the arm of the wheelchair. He tried to wipe it off with his newspaper. Shook his head at the black flecks on Mary-Lou's clothes. Helped to pick eggshell out of Britt's hair. Talked soothingly to both of them.

I sat at the garden table and watched from a distance. Siv and Ruth came pottering by. They'd taken the opportunity for a day at liberty. Now they stopped and clucked for a moment, as if to express a cursory opinion on the scene.

'The worst is over now,' I reassured them with a sigh.

*

Britt soon calmed down. She wasn't one to harbour a grudge. She was certainly impulsive and could flare up and act like an idiot, but she was always quick to repent. She always knew when she'd gone too far. Maybe life had taught her that.

She apologised to Mary-Lou now. Crouched down and put her arm round her. It seemed to me it would have been better if she'd just walked off. If she'd left Mary-Lou to herself.

Mary-Lou was upset. She sat crying silently for a long time. Then she began sobbing loudly and Dad and I went running over and pushed Britt away and sat with her. I think she'd been crying for nearly an hour by the time she finally composed herself.

Dad went in to see Britt and I wondered how he was going to solve this one.

'I want to go home,' said Mary-Lou.

Perhaps that would be best, I thought. Maybe the only right thing to do is for Mary-Lou and me to go back to the city now. Having had the thought I realised that I actually wanted to go back quite badly. There was only a little over a week to go before school started and lots of my mates must be home by now. I might be able to go along to the Stadium and watch our local team play. And take Mary-Lou to the funfair. No, I didn't really fancy that. But I wouldn't mind taking her to the National Gallery. There were a few paintings I'd like to show her.

But I wasn't ready to leave yet. Not right now. Not like this. The summer was worthy of a better ending than this.

'Maybe we should just wait and see,' I said.

Then Dad and Britt came out of the house and I could tell that the peace talks were concluded. They sat down with us.

'Britt and I are going back tomorrow morning,' my father announced. 'I have to work on Sunday anyway. I'll come out next Friday and you can come home with me then.'

'What do you say, Mary-Lou?' I asked.

She thought for a moment. Then simply nodded.

'Good of you, Dad,' I said.

'It'll be rainy at the weekend,' said Britt.

When we were finally on our own again we didn't really know what to do. We stood at the gate listening to Britt's Mazda bumping across the meadow. I heaved a sigh of relief as the noise died away and the gentle breath of the woods took over. Everything was back to normal. Just Mary-Lou and me.

'What do you feel like doing?' I asked.

'Dunno,' she replied.

And I could hear from her tone that things were far from normal again. But I pretended not to notice. I wanted so much for us to make something of these last few days. For everything to be as it was before.

'I wouldn't mind a swim,' I said. 'It's days since my last effort. I wonder if I can still do it. What if it only works on Fjuk!'

But Mary-Lou didn't laugh. She started off towards the house. I walked along beside her.

'Good thing she's gone, anyway,' I said.

'Yes,' Mary-Lou replied.

That was virtually all she said the whole day. I wheeled her around and tried one thing after another, feeling more and more like my father. But nothing made any impact. Nothing seemed to get through to her. I gave up eventually and left her in peace. I took my sketchpad and wandered down to the jetty. I sat cross-legged at the far end. The lake was smooth today, the water translucent right to the bottom. I could see the rippled sand all the way out, the green perch motionless in the shade of the decking, the coal-black alder cones that roll to and fro on the lake-bed when it's windy.

I moved my pencil slowly over the soft sketching paper. Took in all the familiar lines on my horizon. My gaze ranged over Norden Farm and its golden wheatfields, the stony tip of the north point and the square silhouette of Fjuk. The mirage effect was making everything hover slightly. The whole world was on tiptoe.

I worked quite briskly and when I'd finished I studied the result for some time. I thought it was a bit different from the others I'd done. Perhaps there was something else in it, a question or a feeling. What if I'd learnt how to do it at last! But then the usual doubts assailed me and I concluded it was just another of my semi-successful attempts.

Mary-Lou came down to the jetty and wheeled herself along to me. At first she sat silently writing in her eternal notebook diary. Then she took a peek over my shoulder at the sketch I'd done. I'd signed it: *Adam O*. And dated it *5th August*.

'That's brill,' she said.

'Do you think so?'

She reached out for it: 'May I see?'

I gave her the pad and she studied the drawing intently. Then raised her head and examined the lake, as if comparing the reality.

'You draw superbly, Adam. Exactly as it is only better.'

She started leafing through, turning the sheets gently and reflectively. Lingered over each sketch. I remembered when I'd shown her the pad earlier in the summer, how fast and indifferently she'd flicked through. Like when you skim through a newspaper you've already read.

Then I noticed she'd almost reached the part she wasn't supposed to see, so I snatched it back.

'You can't look at any more,' I said. 'The rest is secret.'

'How rotten of you.'

'I'm not being nasty, Mary-Lou, but I have to keep that one to myself until it's ready. Then you can see it.'

'How much longer do you need?'

'Depends on you,' I replied. 'If you felt like sitting, I shouldn't think it would take much longer.'

'How about now?'

'Sure, if you like.'

We sat in our usual place on the beach under the alder trees. It came easily this time. I started straight off and worked without analysing things so much. I knew I'd learnt a lot this summer, both about drawing and about Mary-Lou.

Her face had changed today. Out on Fjuk she was so soft and alive. Dignified and relaxed at the same time. Like a native islander. Or at least how I imagined one to be.

Now there was something else shining in her eyes, a kind of melancholy. I guessed that her mind was back in reality again. In the complicated, grey, daily grind. Everyday life, for better or worse.

I noticed that the variations in her expression no longer bothered me. I knew her face now. I'd somehow learnt how to navigate between all the versions of Mary-Lou that appeared before me. I could finally see through them!

But as I sat there drawing I kept thinking about how a person can vary so much. That the same face can fluctuate from one day to another, from one hour to the next. We might have one look in the morning and a completely different one by the evening. Was it because we were an amalgamation of so many individual people, going back generations? Mary-Lou must be a mixture of her mother and father, Irja and Björn. Of their thoughts, feelings and dreams. She was their dream. But she must also have elements of her maternal and paternal grandmothers, and presumably of her grandfathers, and maybe even a few drops of her great-grandparents.

Have people always been so complex? Or was it getting worse and worse with every new generation, with every divorce?

My head was starting to spin from all this mental activity. I laid down my pencil and stretched my legs. Stood back from my chair to view her better.

Oddly enough that slightly sad expression made her both vulnerable and sweet. I didn't think she'd ever looked prettier. A maxim from school came to mind, something Gunilla Fahlander had said when we were practising painting one another in class, something about always daring to be yourself: *Perfect human beings are totally uninteresting, it's our faults and imperfections that make us exciting.* I think that's roughly what she said. It sounded too artificially concocted then. Now I thought I understood what she meant.

'You look really fab today.'

'Thanks,' was all she said.

'Better than Mona Lisa.'

She laughed – at last!

Afterwards we went in the lake. And it may have been in celebration of the fact that Dad and Britt Börjesson were now halfway to Stockholm that we stripped off all our clothes and slung them up into the dark-green foliage of the alders. Mary-Lou sat in her chair and I was about to wheel her out into the water when she suddenly heaved herself up.

'I want to walk.'

'Okay,' I said.

I helped her out and supported her round the waist as usual. We walked slowly and carefully one step at a time over the baking hot sand. But not as well as before. She kept having to stop, and when we tried to go on her legs just wouldn't. I could see it was a bad day. That it would always be like this: good days and bad days. I picked her up and carried her out into the water till it reached my midriff. Then she wriggled out of my arms and plunged in. I followed her example and dived in, doing some strokes without even thinking about it, but as soon as I realised what my movements were I kept on swimming. I did stroke after stroke, stretching my arms in front of me, kicking out my legs strongly behind. When I felt I'd swum far enough I stood up and held my right arm in the air and yelled, 'Yes! I can swim!'

She laughed so much that she swallowed water and I had to swim over and rescue her. As we very gradually made our way out, the water felt beautifully warm.

'This is the warmest it's been,' she said. 'Ever, I mean.'

'I believe you,' I said. 'It was a good summer to learn to swim.'

I saw a TV series a few years ago where they rang celebrities at home and then just stalked right into their kitchens and opened their fridges and prepared a meal from whatever they found there. They had a proper chef with them but the celebrities had no advance warning. The chef could make a real banquet out of a mildewed cheese and a few wrinkled carrots.

I told Mary-Lou about it as we stood in front of our fridge. She didn't remember having watched it.

'We could do with a chef like that now,' I said.

There was some food there: three packs of bacon, a

large pack of hot dogs, and the mouldy remains of a cooked chicken. And a shrivelled leek in the vegetable compartment. I recognised it because I'd bought it before our trip to Fjuk. Dad and Britt should have thought about what they were stuffing themselves with.

The situation in the larder was much as before. Except that the tins were in neater rows. Every tin in the front row was exactly the same distance from the edge of the shelf. It had to be Britt who'd arranged them. I saw a few new ones for this summer: ravioli and tinned prawns.

'Let's have a party,' said Mary-Lou.

'Good idea,' I replied. 'What sort?'

'An end-of-summer party. It's over now. I think we should celebrate.'

'It's hardly a cause for celebration. It's bloody sad.'

'Not all celebrations need be happy ones.'

This made me think of when my grandmother died. There was a dinner after the funeral. Everyone was wearing their best clothes and eating and drinking and talking and laughing.

'We'll have a memorial feast, then,' I said.

Mary-Lou chortled in delight at the idea.

'We'll have a black tablecloth and candles, black candles.'

'Can you get such things?' I wondered aloud.

'Oh, Adam,' she said in a tone of mock exasperation, 'sometimes you have no imagination at all. We'll paint them, of course.'

'Brilliant,' I said. 'Shall we eat black food too? Burnt haricot beans?'

'Yuck! Gross!'

I scanned the shelves.

'I know, we'll have a sweet feast. There's any amount of tinned fruit here. Pineapples and peaches and fruit cocktail. And I think there are some pears in brandy somewhere.'

Mary-Lou was considering. I could see the idea appealed to her.

'But they're not black,' she said eventually.

'Oh, Mary-Lou,' I sighed. 'We'll paint the tins, of course.'

We both took it for granted that the feast would be out on the jetty. It was the obvious place, our place. But on my way to the outhouse in search of black paint I felt a raindrop on my forehead. I glanced up at the sky and saw that it was half overcast with grey cloud. I shrugged my shoulders. It still seemed impossible to believe it could rain after all that fine weather.

Hunting among Britt's paint cans I caught sight of a roll of black plastic sacks we kept as spares for the rubbish. I tore a couple off. I found a small tin of black paint, the quick-drying sort. Two hours, it said. Perfect. Another splash of rain on my hand on the way back.

'Look,' I said, unrolling the sacks in front of Mary-Lou, 'if we slit them open we'll have a black tablecloth.'

'Hurrah!'

'I think we're going to have to be inside. It looks like rain.'

'Shame,' she said.

250

'It's nice and cosy indoors when it's raining.'

It took some time to organise everything for our memorial ceremony. I lined up the tins of fruit for her to paint on the kitchen table. We wondered what to do about the plates but then decided we didn't need any. We could eat straight out of the tins.

'Wine?' I enquired.

'Black, please.'

I selected a bottle of Moselblümchen and put it on the table. Mary-Lou transformed the bottle with a few swift brush strokes. There weren't all that many wine glasses left in the cupboard because my dad had an almost uncanny ability to break the stems off them when he washed the dishes. We took two old white coffee mugs instead. They were decidedly more sophisticated when they were painted.

When everything was on the table it looked so dramatic that I wished we had a camera.

'We ought to take a picture of it,' I said.

'Draw it,' said Mary-Lou.

'It wouldn't be the same. This is something we should have a photo of.'

'It looks really sombre,' she said.

'The feast will commence in two hours,' I proclaimed.

It got dark early. The rain, of course. But it might be the autumn, too. In fact it felt as if it had just arrived today.

There was a minor mishap as the banquet was about to begin. The black candles were a disaster. They smoked and stank and we had to extinguish them quickly and replace them with white ones. But actually it looked even more stylish with two white candles against all the black.

'These are you and me,' I said to Mary-Lou as I lit them.

She was wearing a sleeveless short black dress. I had found a pair of old black jeans and a navy-blue T-shirt.

We sat down at table. It really felt like a solemn occasion. The rain was heavier. It was teeming down outside the window.

'It's her fault,' said Mary-Lou.

'Rain is quite appropriate for a mourning ceremony,' I said.

'I thought she was going to kill me.'

'Britt goes ballistic like that sometimes. I hated her when I was little. But she doesn't mean any harm. That's just the way she is. Like a bull in a china shop.'

'More like a bulldozer,' said Mary-Lou. 'I hate her anyway.'

'It was fantastic slinging that egg,' I said. 'When I hit her on the head it felt as if I was getting my revenge for a lot of the things she's done.'

Mary-Lou laughed.

'I couldn't believe my eyes when I saw it running down her neck. I'd never have thought you capable of doing something like that.'

'Nor me.'

'There's a lot we don't know about ourselves,' Mary-Lou remarked.

'I'll drink to that!' I said.

We ate out of the tins with our forks. Juice dripped on the black tablecloth. She went mad over the pears in brandy. I pretended not to like them much so she could have most of them.

I studied her surreptitiously as she sat there in her wheelchair. I'd been fooled at first by that chair. It had taken me a long time to recognise that wasn't what it was about. It wasn't her physical handicap that was the problem. Not any more. It was the other injuries she had suffered. The part of her that broke inside when she lost faith in the people who meant everything to her in her childhood world: when the king betrayed the queen and the princess fell ill with grief. It was the discovery of this imperfection that sucked all the strength out of her. But all this was kind of overshadowed by the peculiar chair.

'What are you thinking about?' she asked.

'About you.'

'About me?'

'Yes. And about me.'

'About you and me?'

'Yes. About you and me and pears in brandy and the hermit of Fjuk.'

'About you and me and pears in brandy and the hermit of Fjuk? How do they fit together?'

'They belong together. Now they do, at any rate.'

'Oh.'

'And I think of your dad occasionally too. You ought to see him sometimes, you know.'

She stared out of the window. The rain was running down the panes on the outside and the inside was misted up from our breath. We couldn't see anything, and nothing could see us.

'I know,' she said eventually. 'I will. But not just yet.'

'Because he doesn't want to?'

'Yes. Because he doesn't want to and because I don't want to.'

'I'm not sure you're right,' I said. 'It's obvious he'd like to meet up with you.'

'I suppose so. But he needs a chance to sort his own life out first. To sort himself out. That's what I think he means.'

'Seeing you might help,' I suggested.

'He's ashamed of the way he's living now.'

'And you let him carry on thinking like that. You don't do anything to change the situation either.'

'He's got a drink problem, Adam!'

'There's nothing unusual in that. Masses of people drink. But he's your father.'

She didn't answer. It was a naff thing to say. I felt the need to explain myself.

'Some grown-ups are exactly like children. Inside, that is. They're just as small, and have the same strong feelings and the same weaknesses. Experience the same pleasure, the same painful misery. Take Britt Börjesson, for example, she...'

'Do we have to keep talking about her!'

'We're not talking about her. We're talking about you and your father.'

The last part of our time together was nothing like the rest of the summer. It rained. When it stopped one afternoon I went to the John Bauer forest to look for mushrooms. I just managed to get there before it started again.

Mary-Lou mostly sat indoors. The chicken run was left open, but Siv and Ruth didn't want to go out either.

I went down and bailed out the boat, which was full of rainwater. The deck boards were floating around in the cockpit. I had a totally different view of it when stepping aboard now. I hadn't been fully aware of it before. To me it was just a simple rowing boat like any number of others. Now it was the *Black Gull*, the ship of adventure.

It was hard to get on with the portrait of Mary-Lou in this weather. We tried indoors. She sat in the kitchen but it wouldn't come right. I ought really to be able to finish it without her. It was all in my head now.

I completed the willowherb and the background.

It occurred to me that maybe we should call on Björn anyway, but I didn't suggest it. I had to remind myself it wasn't that simple.

Then Mary-Lou said, 'I want to go home now.'

'My dad's coming out on Friday.'

'I want to go before then, Adam. I want to go now.'

I pedalled over to the supermarket to phone her mother. It was drizzling. When I got there I discovered I'd forgotten the phone card. I had no money either, but my good friend Linda said I could have a card on credit.

'You can come in and pay another day.'

'That's really kind of you, Linda.'

Taking the card from her, I realised it was the first time I'd looked at her properly. She smiled at me. A little shyly. She had beautiful eyes.

'Thanks,' I said. 'I'll be back.'

Irja wasn't at home and I hesitated for several seconds as the answerphone began the usual patter about there unfortunately being nobody there to speak to you right now but that you were welcome to leave a message. It was Mary-Lou's voice and it felt bizarre to be listening to her there when I knew she was here.

I took a deep breath and said, 'Hi, this is Adam, I wonder if you'd mind coming to fetch Mary-Lou because she wants to go home now. We've had a wonderful time and...well, that's all really. I hope you'll hear this and that you can collect her...'Bye, then...Oh, Mary-Lou sends her love...'Bye.'

The rain had finally stopped when I cycled back. But there was a strong head wind.

Irja arrived at lunchtime the next day. She didn't have the midnight-blue Golf but a yellow Renault Mégane. I hardly recognised her. She looked younger and smarter. Vivacious in a way. She was wearing a red dress and black shoes and her eyes seemed sort of compelling.

'Hello, Adam. It's nice to see you again.'

'Nice to see you too.'

She hugged Mary-Lou and bent over her and the wheelchair for some time, including them both in the hug.

'Would you like something to eat?' I asked.

'Is there anything?'

I thought for a moment.

'Prawn omelette?'

'That would be lovely.'

While I prepared the meal she walked round the garden with Mary-Lou. From the window I could see Mary-Lou showing her various things. They stood watching Siv and Ruth for a while. The sun appeared and I went out and dried off the garden furniture with a cloth and laid the table there. I made a tomato and cucumber salad.

Irja said it tasted wonderful.

'Adam's a real chef,' said Mary-Lou. 'And an artist. He's done a portrait of me, but it's not quite ready yet.'

'I remember you were good at drawing even as a little boy,' said Irja.

I stood up and went into the cottage. I came out with the picture for Mary-Lou. I'd wrapped it in newspaper and tied it up with string.

'You're finished now,' I said. 'I completed you last night.'

Then we parted. I helped to carry her things to the car. Mary-Lou held her package pressed tight to her chest. I said we'd probably see one another in town. But I suspected both of us had the feeling we might not meet again. Not like this summer anyway. We'd had something to sort out together. It was done now. We couldn't do any more for each other.

I wish it hadn't been like this. I wish there had been a different ending. A happier ending, as in a film. But life isn't always like that.

5

The following year Björn sold Norden Farm and moved to Stockholm. My dad heard from Irja that he was living in an apartment in the western suburb of Fittja and that he and Mary-Lou had started meeting up again.

I had a Christmas card from her. She wrote on it that she'd had the portrait framed and that she was very pleased with it. She also said she was going to study abroad for a year, in France, and was looking forward to that.

I kept her gold visiting card on the wall of my room. I rang once but got the answerphone.

I wasn't sure what I was going to do myself. I still had doubts about whether I was good enough to be an artist. I sometimes thought of the hermit of Fjuk.

Life was back to normal again. Even though it hadn't seemed as if it ever would be that summer when Mary-Lou threw herself out of her cherry tree.

I never could bring myself to ask her about it. It didn't seem so important afterwards. I was inclined to agree with my father that it might have been an accident after all.

Life went on. It does, despite everything.